# THE LITTLE DRAGON

### BY

### BETTY NEELS

MILLS & BOON®

First published in Great Britain 1978
Large Print Edition 2006
Harlequin Mills & Boon Limited,
Eton House, 18-24 Paradise Road,
Richmond, Surrey TW9 1SR

© Betty Neels

ISBN-13: 978 0 263 19307 7
ISBN-10:      0 263 19307 1

Set in Times Roman 16½ on 18 pt.
16-0706-51675

Printed and bound in Great Britain
by Antony Rowe Ltd, Chippenham, Wiltshire

# CHAPTER ONE

IT WAS starting to snow; the feathery flakes fell soundlessly in a kind of slow motion, turning the old-fashioned gabled houses lining the canal into a painting by Pieter de Hoogh.

The girl at the window stood quietly, staring down at the people in the streets below as they bustled to and fro over the narrow arched bridge in front of the house, intent on getting home before the weather worsened. She was a pretty girl, small and slim with nut-brown hair and wide grey eyes heavily fringed. Her nose turned up the merest trifle and her mouth was too wide, although it curved enchantingly. She looked happy too, which was surprising, for Constantia Morley, twenty-six years old and an orphan for twenty of those years, hadn't a great deal to be happy about.

She had been brought up by an aunt, unmarried and straitlaced, who had tried in vain to make Constantia straitlaced too and quite failed; but she had been kind to her niece after her fashion, and educated her well and raised no objection when Constantia evinced a desire to become a nurse. She had died a year after her niece had taken her finals, and because she had overlooked the fact that the will she had made many years earlier held no provision for Constantia, she had left her nothing at all. The modest amount she had left went to various charities, and the house to some distant relation Constantia had never heard of, who, taking possession of it with almost indecent haste, couldn't wait to show Constantia the door.

From then on Constantia had lived at the hospital where she worked, on the fringe of London, with plenty of friends with whom to spend her free time but no home or family to visit. But she wasn't sorry for herself; self-pity wasn't going to help her to make her way in life, and if she were lucky one day she would marry and have a family of her own. Indeed, she had had several proposals during the last few years, but although she had liked the proposers well enough, none of them had swept her off her feet, and she wanted to be swept off her feet...

By the time she had reached her twenty-sixth birthday she was beginning to wonder if she was expecting too much of life, and egged on by a restlessness she couldn't understand, she gave up her post as Sister on the medical wards, and went into private nursing. She had been told at the time that it wasn't the life for her; she was a good nurse and used to hard work and the pressures of a busy ward; she would be bored. But she hadn't been bored, although she was willing to concede the fact that life wasn't all roses.

She had had a variety of patients during the last six months, spending the first few weeks in a Scottish castle miles from anywhere, followed by a mercifully brief period in a remote Welsh cottage with no telephone, a very sick patient and only a deaf old woman for company. Then there had been a wholesale grocer in the Midlands who worried unceasingly about his money, and then a small spoilt girl in Bournemouth and a charming old lady in a London flat. And now here she was in Holland with what she had to admit was the worst patient of the lot.

She turned away from the window at last; her sharp eyes had seen Doctor Sperling's Renault coming over the bridge. He would be at the house in a few moments now and she must go down and meet him in the hall. It was one of her patient's little foibles that Constantia should always be waiting for the doctor; she had to wear uniform too, which, when she considered how little nursing there was to do, seemed ridiculous. She suspected that she was a prestige symbol and that her cap and apron were needed to substantiate her patient's boasting.

She reached the dark hall just as Nel, the elderly maid, opened the door and the doctor entered.

He was a man of middle age, tall and balding and, Constantia had to admit, as fussy as an old woman. He greeted her with a condescension which made her grit her small even teeth, remarked on the inclemency of the weather: 'It is, after all, the last day of February,' he informed her in the manner of someone handing out vital information, and then, divested of his coat and hat: 'You will lead the way to your patient, nurse?'

He had said that each day for just over a week and she had answered, just as she had done each time he came, 'Of course, Doctor,' and led the way upstairs again to her patient's room.

Mrs Dowling was lying on a day bed drawn up to the old-fashioned stove. She was a thin woman, made even thinner by the diet she had insisted upon keeping to until it was discovered that she was a diabetic. Her hair was grey, curly and short and her features strong, with a perpetual expression of annoyance upon them. Her voice was loud, penetrating and bossy.

She responded to the doctor's greeting with a languid nod and broke at once into complaint. 'You really must explain to Nurse, Doctor Sperling, that I am quite capable of compiling my own diet.' She didn't look at Constantia as she spoke, indeed she could have been invisible. 'And you must do something about my headaches.'

Doctor Sperling put his fingertips together and looked wise. He said, in almost perfect English: 'Dear lady, your condition, unless controlled by insulin, would be cause of those headaches. You must allow me to guide you in the matter. I will discuss your diet with Nurse and see what alternatives there are to the diet I prescribed. And now you must tell me how you feel today, Mrs Dowling.'

His patient spoke at some length, her voice grating unpleasantly on Constantia's ear. But she had heard it all before, so she felt justified in allowing her thoughts to wander. Tomorrow, she reflected, she would have the half day Mrs Dowling so grudgingly gave her twice a week. She had glimpsed the town briefly already, now she was going to explore it; its churches, museums, old houses, canals and narrow alleys. After all, she might never have the chance to come to Delft again. She was really very lucky, she could have been up to her eyes on Women's Medical...the Nieuw Kerk first, she decided, and then the Town Hall...

Mrs Dowling had paused for breath; Constantia switched her mind back to her present surroundings, and although she wasn't required to speak, looked intelligent.

Ten minutes later she was attending Doctor Sperling to the door. The new diet had been discussed, written down and approved by the patient. The insulin doses the doctor had tactfully left until he was alone with Constantia; she listened carefully to his instructions and smiled a goodbye, quite sorry for him because although he was well thought of by his colleagues in the medical profession and had a fashionable practice, he still had to suffer the tiresomeness of patients like Mrs Dowling. And it seemed as though he would have to suffer her for some time yet, for she harboured the notion that her complaint was something she could ignore if she wished, and indeed before the doctor had persuaded her to have a private nurse she had played ducks and drakes with both her diet and her insulin.

She hadn't liked the idea of a nurse at first, but after the beginnings of a diabetic coma, luckily nipped in the bud by the doctor, she had changed her views and even got a good deal of satisfaction from having a nurse to look after her. She had a number of friends, hard-faced women like herself who were addicted to bridge and the bullying of those they considered beneath them, and as none of them had had a private nurse at any time, she derived a good deal of satisfaction from Constantia's presence. But not pleasure; she had tried in vain to bully her, but Constantia wasn't to be cowed. She had learned to show an imperturbable front which quite disconcerted her patient, and although she had a nasty temper upon occasion, she kept it well in check.

The agency for whom she worked had thought that she might be in Holland for two or three weeks, no longer, but already a week had gone by and if Mrs Dowling was going to insist on doing exactly what she liked about her diet, then Constantia could see that she might be there for very much longer. Given a sensible patient, the diabetes could have been controlled within two weeks, diets worked out and the insulin doses adjusted, so that an occasional visit to the doctor would have been quite sufficient. But Mrs Dowling wasn't sensible, she was also very rich and moreover suffered from the illusion that money would and could smooth her path. Quite why she needed Constantia was a puzzle, and certainly she had said nothing about her leaving. Constantia, who liked to nurse patients who needed all her skill and care, felt impatient when she thought about it—but if she were to go, the chances were that Mrs Dowling would do something silly like eating éclairs for tea and forgetting her insulin, and end up in hospital in a coma.

Constantia went back upstairs and spent the next half an hour persuading her patient that *Vienne snitczels* just wouldn't do for her dinner that evening.

'I sometimes wish that I were back in England,' complained Mrs Dowling. 'I could go to one of those health hydros where I'm sure my wishes would be carried out.'

'Well, there's no reason why you shouldn't,' said Constantia briskly, 'if you want to.'

Her patient cast her a look of dislike. 'When I want your opinion I'll ask for it,' she snapped. 'What have you to offer in place of *Vienne snitczels*?'

Constantia was ready with quite a list; Mrs Dowling rejected first one and then the other and then finally, seeing that Constantia had no intention of ordering the *snitczels*, graciously allowed that Parma ham cut wafer-thin might do very well. Constantia retired to the kitchen to confer with the cook and on the way back again lingered for a moment at a downstairs window.

The snow was coming down thickly now and it was almost dark. Across the bridge she could see the shops lighted up; it would be pleasant to wrap up warmly and explore—tomorrow she would do just that.

By lunch time the next day the snow had ceased and the sun had come out; it was cold, though. Constantia, already a little late because Mrs Dowling had thought up first one and then the other small task for her to do before she went, hurried along the Wijn Haven, across the bridge and into Oude Langen Dijke, where she turned off to cross the market square in the direction of the Nieuwe Kerk. She paused as she went to turn and stare at the Stadhuis; it looked beautiful in its snowy setting—seventeenth-century Baroque, although there was a small part of it which was much older and no longer open to the public. She shivered as she stood; the wind was cold and her coat, several winters old now, wasn't quite adequate. She dismissed the coat with a cheerful shrug and continued on her way, and it was as she reached the far side of the market square that she saw Doctor Sperling's car parked opposite the Nieuwe Kerk. There was another car close by, a shabby little Fiat parked rather carelessly, and its occupant was apparently talking to Doctor Sperling, for she could see that he was talking to someone bending down at his car's window. She had almost reached it when the doctor turned round, saw her, and raised a dignified hand.

Constantia hadn't much dignity. She skipped up to the car and said, 'Hullo, Doctor Sperling,' with an almost childlike friendliness, and then uttered a surprised 'Oh,' as whoever it was on the other side straightened up to look at her over the car's roof. A very large, tall man with pale hair silvering over the temples, his eyes were blue, and heavy-lidded, his nose high-bridged above a large firm mouth. A nice face, decided Constantia, and smiled widely at him.

He had a nice smile too, she discovered. The arm he stretched over the car's roof was enormous, so was his hand, but his grip was gentle. 'Jeroen van der Giessen.' His voice was deep and placid.

'Constantia Morley...' Doctor Sperling's pedantic voice interrupted her. 'Miss Morley is nursing Mrs Dowling.' He poked his head further out of the car window. 'You have a free afternoon, Nurse?'

'It's my half day—I'm exploring, Doctor Sperling.' She smiled at him, delighted with her freedom; she smiled at the large man, too, rather shyly. 'I don't want to miss a minute,' she explained. 'Goodbye, Doctor—Mijnheer van der Giessen.'

She crossed the road and went into the Nieuwe Kerk and Doctor Sperling watching her, observed severely: 'A good nurse, very thorough and conscientious, but one feels that she should take life more seriously.'

'Why?' asked his companion, his eyes on Constantia's small brisk person as it disappeared into the church.

Doctor Sperling coughed. 'She is twenty-six,' he remarked severely.

Two lazy blue eyes twinkled down at him. 'I'm thirty-nine myself and I have the greatest difficulty in taking life seriously.'

The older man examined his nails. 'I'm not surprised, Jeroen, with three children and those dogs and that great house.' He sounded faintly envious. 'And your work.' He sighed. 'I must get on, I've another patient to visit. We must have an evening together…'

'Give me a ring.' The two men shook hands and Doctor Sperling watched the other man insert his giant-like proportions into the Fiat and drive away. He was a good driver; no fiddling with mirrors or gears, no anxious ear cocked for engine noises, just in and away. 'He could drive a biscuit tin,' muttered Doctor Sperling, and drove off himself, only rather more sedately.

Constantia, in between a close study of the stained glass windows in the choir, the Royal Burial Vault of the House of Orange and the mausoleum of William of Orange, allowed her thoughts to dwell upon the man she had just met. She had liked him and he had looked at her as though he had known her already…

She paused to gaze at the great organ. He would be married, of course, with children and from the look of his car, not much money. She wondered what he did for a living and what his wife was like, and then dismissed him from her thoughts and concentrated on the organ. But Jeroen van der Giessen popped back into her head again as she made her way down the church to the door once more. It was a pity that just once in a while one met someone one could feel completely at ease with and then never saw again.

She saw him the minute she went through the door; he was striding across the Markt square, his hands in the pockets of his rather deplorable sheepskin jacket. He reached the road at the same time as she did and said at once: 'Hullo again. How far have you got with the sightseeing?'

'Just the Nieuwe Kerk,' she told him happily, aware that she was glad to see him. 'I'm going over to the Oude Kerk now.'

'Yes? I've an hour to spare, I wondered if you would like to see the Steen—the tower of the Stadhuis, you know. It's a good deal older than the rest of the building—fifteenth century, it was a small museum but it had to close because of staff difficulties, but I know the curator—if you're interested we could go there now, and you could explore the Nieuwe Kerk another time.' He added casually: 'How many half days do you get in a week?'

'Two. I'd love to see the Steen, but are you—can you spare the time?'

'I've an hour, as I said. I like to be home at four o'clock for the children. I usually have visits in the afternoon, but I did them early.'

'You're a doctor?' And when he nodded, 'How many children have you?'

'Three, two boys and a girl. But they're not mine, they're my sister's—she's away for a few months and I've got them with me.'

It was ridiculous to feel so relieved. When he added: 'I'm not married,' Constantia smiled widely. 'Oh—how do you manage, then?'

He shrugged enormous shoulders. 'It isn't for very long—three or four months.' They were walking across the Markt towards the Raadhuis, not hurrying their steps. 'And how do you enjoy looking after Mrs Dowling?'

'You know her?'

'Oh, yes—not as a friend, though.'

'Well then, I can tell you, can't I? I don't enjoy it at all, but I love being here in Delft, so that makes up for it.'

'Makes up for what?'

'Mrs Dowling is rather a difficult patient,' she said carefully, and listened to his bellow of laughter.

'My dear young lady, that is the understatement of the year. Does she still change her diet at every opportunity?'

'Oh, yes.' Constantia stopped to look up at him and thought what a kind face he had. 'But I'm sorry for her too. She's rich, you know, and miserable with it.'

He stared down at her, smiling faintly. 'You think that being rich makes one miserable?'

'I don't know exactly, how should I? I've never been rich, but I don't think wealthy people have much fun...'

'You wouldn't marry a rich man?'

She shook her head. 'They worry about their money, don't they? When I marry, if my husband wants to worry, then I'd like him to worry about me.'

'You don't mind having no money, then?'

'No.' She paused and added seriously: 'Isn't it funny the way we're talking, just as though we've known each other for years and years.'

He said easily, 'Oh, I'm a great believer in instant friendship.' They had reached the Stadhuis and he ushered her up the steps and in through the door to a marble hall; the great staircase faced the door and there were a number of much smaller doors in the walls. Doctor van der Giessen knocked on one of them and poked his head round it to speak to someone in the room beyond. Constantia stood patiently listening to the unintelligible conversation, and wished she could understand just a little of it;

if she were to stay much longer she would start to learn.

Her companion opened the door a little wider and an elderly bearded face peered round it at her, smiled, nodded and disappeared again. 'We can potter,' her guide informed her.

They climbed the stairs together and he showed her the Council Chamber and waited patiently while she admired the view from its windows, and then the portraits of the members of the House of Orange on its walls before leading her to the Wedding Chamber. Constantia, athirst for information, asked: 'Does everyone have to get married here?'

'Oh, yes—it isn't legal otherwise.'

'But what about church? I shouldn't feel married…'

Doctor van der Giessen smiled a little. 'A number of people are married in church too. A twice tied knot, one might say.' He put a hand on her arm. 'Come and see the Steen Tower.'

It seemed that he was a privileged visitor and she was glad of it; the Steen Tower proved to house a small museum, closed for the time being to the public, the contents of which—to do with the law of the land—her companion explained in a leisurely manner. As they were leaving the Stadhuis at length, he asked: 'Tea? There's a small teashop just across the Markt.'

He gave her a placid smile and she thought again what a nice man he was and how easy she felt with him. 'I'd love some, but do you have the time?'

'Oh, yes. I've no surgery until half-past five.'

'The children?'

'Playing with friends after school—they'll be brought home.'

She smiled widely at him. 'Well then—' They started to walk across the Markt. 'What a lovely half day I'm having,' she told him happily.

He beamed down at her. 'Yes? And I—it is very pleasant to show one's home town to someone who is really interested in it.'

They had reached a small corner shop, a pastry cook's she had thought, but through it was a very small room with tables and chairs, quite empty. They had their tea and Constantia ate a cream cake with real pleasure. 'For,' she explained, 'Mrs Dowling mustn't have any-thing like this—I have to eat the same food as she does.'

Her companion looked astonished. 'But she's on a diabetic diet, is she not?'

Constantia nodded. 'Yes—I have sugar in my tea and coffee, of course. But no cake or biscuits or puddings.'

The doctor muttered something in Dutch and she said severely: 'That sounded rude.'

He laughed. 'It was. Have another cake—your carbohydrates must be at a very low ebb.'

She speared a second luscious confection. 'Yes, I thought that too. I'm being greedy. You've not eaten anything.' It occurred to her suddenly that perhaps he hadn't very much money—three children would cost a lot to feed and he had a dreadful old car. On the other hand, when he had taken off his sheepskin jacket, she had noticed that the grey suit he was wearing was of very fine cloth and most elegantly cut. Of course, being such a size he would have to have his clothes made for him, just as he would have to present a well-tailored person to his patients. Probably he bought a very expensive suit every five years or so. It worried her a little and she said presently: 'It is kind of you to give me tea—I mean, we've only just met, and you didn't have to...if we'd been old friends or not seen each other for a long time...'

He smiled lazily at her. 'I hope we'll soon be old friends, and I have the strangest feeling that I have known you for a very long time.'

'That's funny—I felt like that too when we met. Perhaps we've met before and haven't re-membered.' She poured more tea for them both. 'Do you ever go to London?'

'Yes—from time to time.'

'Well, perhaps that's it? St Anne's isn't a very big hospital, but it specialises in defi-ciency diseases and diabetes and metabolism.'

'And do you plan to go back there?'

She shook her head. 'Oh, no, I thought I'd do private nursing for a year because one can really save money, and then I shall go to Can-ada or New Zealand.'

'Your family don't mind?' he asked.

'I haven't a family. I can only just remember my parents. An aunt brought me up; she died a year or two ago. There isn't anyone else.'

'No boy-friend?'

'No.'

He leaned back in his chair and looked at her thoughtfully. 'I'm surprised. Don't you approve of us?'

She had to laugh. 'Of course I do, only I've never met anyone I wanted to marry. I expect I shall one day.'

'I expect you will, too. In the meantime you have Mrs Dowling to contend with.' He took a pipe from his pocket. 'Would you mind if I smoked?'

'Not a bit.' She savoured the last crumbs of her cake. 'I should be going.'

'You have a half day—surely you can stay out as long as you wish?'

'Oh, yes, of course. I wasn't going back to Mrs Dowling. There's an organ recital at the Walloon church—I thought I'd go.'

'And until then?' he prompted.

'Well, I want to look at the shops and learn my way about the town.' She picked up her gloves and began to put them on. 'I have enjoyed my afternoon. Thank you very much, Doctor van der Giessen.'

She stifled quick disappointment at his non-committal, 'That sounds very pleasant,' and when she got up he rose to his feet too with no sign of reluctance—and there was no reason why he should do otherwise, she told herself sensibly.

All the same, the rest of her half day seemed flat. Constantia had faced loneliness for several years now, quite cheerfully, too, but now she felt lonely. As she prepared for bed later she decided it was because she hadn't met anyone—any man—with whom she had felt so relaxed. Probably she would see him again from time to time, but she would have to take care not to go out of her way to do so. He had been kind because she was a stranger in Delft and he had wanted her to see something of it. He would be a very good friend, she thought sleepily; impersonal friendliness among the young men she had known had been a rarity...

She closed her eyes, content with her day, and then opened them again as Mrs Dowling's bell pinged in her ear. Constantia stifled a yawn, put on her dressing gown and slippers, and went along to the large room at the front of the house. Mrs Dowling always rang when she had had a half day; probably to make her pay for her free time. Constantia made a charmingly naughty face and opened the door.

'There you are,' declared her patient, quite unnecessarily. 'I can't sleep—I'll have a cup of tea. What did you do with yourself?'

'Oh, I had a delightful afternoon,' Constantia told her happily, and went away to make the tea.

# CHAPTER TWO

CONSTANTIA SAW Doctor van der Giessen three days later, on a rather bleak Sunday afternoon, because Mrs Dowling had decided that it suited her to allow Constantia to have her half day then...that there would be very little for her to do hadn't entered her patient's head. She was having friends in for tea and bridge, and there would be no need for her company.

So Constantia wrapped herself up in her winter coat once more and went for a walk. The Hotel Central would be open, she would have tea there and then go back and write letters and perhaps spend an hour conning the Dutch phrase book she had purchased; and if the walk palled, there were two museums which would be open until five o'clock. She had been saving them for a wet day, but they would pass a pleasant hour.

She was making her way towards the Nieuwe Plantage when she saw the doctor coming towards her. He wasn't alone; there were three small children skipping around him and two magnificent long-haired Alsatian dogs were at his heels, and trotting along on a lead, a small black and white dog of no known parentage.

'Another half day?' asked the doctor as they drew level with her and came to a halt.

'Yes. Mrs Dowling is playing bridge this afternoon.'

'We were just saying that we would like something nice to happen—and here you are.'

'Well,' began Constantia, 'you're very kind to say so.'

'Paul,' he introduced the elder of the two boys, 'and Pieter, seven and nine years old, and Elisabeth—she's five.'

The children shook hands and smiled at her. They were nice-looking and very clean and neat; she wondered how the doctor managed that.

'And the dogs—Solly and Sheba, and this...' He indicated the nondescript animal now worrying his shoes, 'is Prince.'

Constantia stroked three silky heads and said 'Hullo,' and the doctor observed: 'Good, now you know everyone. We're on our way back from the usual Sunday afternoon walk.' He paused and went on smoothly: 'We mustn't keep you—your free time is precious.'

Constantia's tongue almost tripped over itself in her hurry to agree. Not for the world would she have admitted, even to herself, that she would have welcomed a few minutes spent in the doctor's company, not to mention the children and the dogs. She bade them all a cheerful goodbye and walked off in a purposeful fashion as though she really had somewhere to go. She longed to look round and watch them on their way home, but if one of them happened to look round at the same time, they might think that she was being nosey.

She walked on, not seeing her surroundings at all; they would be home by now—a small, shabby house, probably, if the car was anything to go by, but it would be cosy inside and

they would have tea round the fire and do jigsaw puzzles and draw, and the doctor would
sit in his chair and admire the children's efforts
and catch up on his reading when he wasn't
called upon to help with the jigsaw puzzle...
She made herself think about something else;
it was only because she felt a little lonely that
she was allowing her imagination to run away
with her, and she had better hurry back to the
town's centre or the museums would be
closed. There might be a café open where she
could get a cup of tea.

She couldn't find a caf, but she did discover
the Hofje van Elisabeth Pauw, a cluster of
almshouses round a courtyard, old and peace-
ful and delightful to see even on a cold March
afternoon. And as the Hofje van Gratie was
close by it seemed a shame not to take a look
at it while she was in that part of the town. By
the time she had found her way back to the
Markt square, it was too late to visit a museum; she went instead to the Hotel Central
and had coffee in its dim warmth. There were
a lot of people there, sitting in family groups
or couples with their heads close together; it

gave her the illusion that she was one of them, so that she settled quite happily to writing the postcards she bought at the bar and presently ordered more coffee and a *ham broodje* to go with it. Nel would have kept some supper for her—soup and something cold which she was expected to take to her room on a tray.

The house was quiet as she went in an hour later. Constantia started gingerly up the stairs, intent on gaining her room without Mrs Dowling knowing that she was back. A half day was a half day, after all, although her patient seemed to think that once she was in the house, she could resume her duties at the drop of a hat. She had gained the landing when Mrs Dowling's harsh voice called: 'Is that you, Nurse? Come in here.'

Constantia sighed and turned her steps to the front of the house where Mrs Dowling spent so much of her day. That lady looked up from her book as she went in with a peevish: 'I can't think what you find to do, Nurse—you might just as well stay in the house.'

'I find exploring Delft very interesting, Mrs Dowling.'

'Huh—and who do you meet on the sly?' Mrs Dowling suddenly smiled rather nastily. 'So you do meet someone—I can see it in your face.'

'No, Mrs Dowling, I don't, not an arranged meeting, and that's what you're hinting at. I did meet someone this afternoon—we said good afternoon and that was all.'

'Who was it?' demanded her patient.

'I don't think it could be of any interest to you, but there's no secret about it. Doctor van der Giessen—I met him with Doctor Sperling a day or so ago.'

'Him—he hasn't any money,' said Mrs Dowling deliberately.

Constantia's grey eyes surveyed her with veiled contempt. 'He's a hardworking doctor—surely that's more important?'

Her patient made a vulgar noise. 'And what use is that with three children to clothe and feed and educate? I don't know him, but Doctor Sperling has hinted as much. He's poor.' She uttered the word with contempt.

Constantia composed her features into mild interest and said: 'Oh?'

'Don't tell me you haven't made it your business to find out? I thought all nurses were after doctors. Well, now you do know, so there's no point in making eyes at him.'

Constantia went a little pale; she said evenly: 'If you'll excuse me, Mrs Dowling, I still have an hour or so of my half day—I have some letters to write. I'll say goodnight.'

'You're so damned ladylike!' snapped her patient.

She had spoilt what was left of the day, of course. Constantia went along to the kitchen and collected her frugal supper and then went to bed early, for there was nothing else to do. She took great care not to think about Doctor van der Giessen at all.

Doctor Sperling came the next morning and because Mrs Dowling complained of headache, prescribed tablets—to be fetched by Constantia immediately, for the *apotheek* would be unable to deliver them at once. 'Just over the bridge,' he told her, 'go through the shopping precinct, you will find it a little further along. You will need to get there by noon—they will be closing for lunch.'

Mrs Dowling glanced at the diamond-studded watch on her bony wrist. 'Yes, go now, Nurse, and you, Doctor Sperling, can stay for a few minutes and see what is to be done about my diet. I need variety—my appetite needs tempting.'

Constantia felt a pang of pity for Doctor Sperling as she slipped away. Even ten minutes away from her patient was a pleasurable little bonus. Not even that lady's 'Hurry back, Nurse,' could dim that. She whipped off the cap Mrs Dowling insisted that she wore, fetched her coat and let herself out of the house.

She had finished her errand and was almost at the bridge when Doctor van der Giessen, carrying his bag, came out of a doorway.

His 'Good morning' was genial. 'Free so early in the day?' he wanted to know.

She beamed at him warmly, for it was like meeting an old friend. 'No, just an errand—some pills for Mrs Dowling; Doctor Sperling wanted her to have them at once.' She gave a small skip. 'I have to be very quick.'

He was blocking her path and he made no move to stand aside.

'It's not good for you to rush around. I prescribe two minutes of standing just where you are—we can while them away with a little light conversation. Did you enjoy your half day?'

'Oh—yes. I walked to the Hofje van Elisabeth Pauw and then I went to see the other one close by, and by then it was too late to go to a museum, so I had coffee at the Central Hotel—it's nice there. There were a lot of people.'

His eyes were quick to see the wistfulness on her face. He said gently: 'And then what did you do?'

'I went back...' She remembered Mrs Dowling's remarks and went bright pink.

'And your patient was waiting for you?' he prompted.

'Yes, she was—but it didn't matter.' She smiled at him. 'I really must go.'

He fell into step beside her, and as they crossed the bridge asked: 'When is your next half day?'

'Thursday. There's a bridge party. It's market day, isn't it? I'm going to have a super time going round the stalls.'

He caught her arm in a casual grip and steered her across the busy street. 'I have a half day too—perhaps we could go together.'

They were on the pavement outside the Hotel Central's coffee room, full of people sitting at the little tables in its windows, watching the street and the passers-by in it.

'Oh, I'd love that.' Constantia sounded like a happy child, 'but wouldn't it bore you?'

He was looking at the curious faces peering at them through the glass, but he turned to look down at her. 'No, it wouldn't. I enjoy your company.' He smiled in a friendly fashion and went on casually: 'I'll be here waiting for you.'

'Two o'clock,' pronounced Constantia, and added, 'You have no idea how marvellous it is to have a friend.'

'You think of me as a friend?' There was mild interest in his voice.

'Oh, yes. I hope you don't mind?'

'I'm delighted. Shall we shake on it?' They shook hands and the interested faces on the other side of the glass window smiled, although neither of them noticed that.

Constantia was late. Mrs Dowling made a point of pointing that out to her. She grumbled on and off for the rest of the day too, so that Constantia went to bed with a faint headache; not that that mattered. Thursday wasn't too far away; she would wash her hair, she decided rather absurdly, and fell to wondering if she should have it cut short and permed—perhaps not, supposing it didn't suit her? Unlike most pretty girls, she had never considered herself more than passable—although it doesn't matter what one looks like to a friend, she reminded herself, and that was what Doctor van der Giessen was.

Thursday held a touch of spring, with a brilliant sunshine making nonsense of the biting wind. Constantia, tempted to wear a thin wool dress under her winter coat, changed her mind and put on a Marks and Spencer sweater and a pleated skirt and tied a scarf round her slender neck. No one would see what she was wearing under her coat and the dress wouldn't be thick enough. She pulled a knitted cap down over her ears and thus sensibly attired, hurried from the house before Mrs Dowling, awaiting her friends for bridge in the sitting room, should think of something for her to do.

The doctor was waiting, bare-headed in the wind and not seeming to mind. He greeted her casually and she said at once: 'Sorry I'm a bit late—it's sometimes difficult to get away.' And then: 'You're sure you don't mind coming to the market? Are the children at school?'

He nodded. 'Though I must get back about half past three or four—they'll be coming home then.'

Less than two hours, she thought regretfully, and then chided herself for being discontented. Two hours was quite a long time and she was lucky to have someone to go out with.

The market square, when they reached it, was teeming with people; housewives with bulging shopping baskets, old men peering at the stalls and buying nothing, children weaving in and out between the grown-ups, dogs barking, and a number of respectable matrons in frightful felt hats and expensive unfashionable coats, who peered at the stalls' contents

with sharp eyes and when they bought anything, bargained for it shrewdly. There weren't
just fruit and vegetable stalls, butchers and
fishmongers and household goods, there were
stalls devoted entirely to cheese, mountains of
it—brightly coloured aprons and dresses and
trestle tables laid out with rows of old-
fashioned corsets and bras. Constantia, her fas-
cinated eyes held by the sight of them, was
quite taken aback.

'They're so large and there are so many,'
she remarked to her companion. 'Whoever
buys them?'

He grinned down at her. 'I've never dared
to stay long enough to find out,' he told her,
'but they must do a roaring trade. As far as I
can remember they haven't changed their—
er—shape since I was a small boy.'

Constantia giggled and then sighed with
pleasure. 'Isn't this a simply gorgeous place?'
she wanted to know. 'And look at those flowers—it's only March and there's roses and lilac
and freesias and tulips…'

'But this isn't the flower market, that's in the Hippolytusbuurt—we'll go there presently.'

They strolled round, the doctor's hand on her arm, for there was a good deal of good-natured pushing and shoving and as he pointed out, her small slim person would have stood very little chance of staying upright. Constantia, who was remarkably tough despite her fairy-like appearance, didn't argue the point; it was pleasant to be looked after so carefully. And the flower market was something she wouldn't have missed for the world, for the stalls lined the whole length of the canal, a riot of spring flowers. Constantia stood and sniffed their fragrance and exclaimed, 'Oh, I've never seen anything like this—are they here all the year round?'

'Yes, even in midwinter. They hang out little orange-coloured lanterns so that the customers can see.' They had paused before a stall and Jeroen van der Giessen spoke to the stall-holder, who smiled and began bunching narcissi, daffodils and tulips in a vast colourful bouquet. When the doctor took them from her and handed them to Constantia she said in utter surprise, 'For me? all these? there are dozens... How absolutely super!'

She couldn't help but see the notes the doctor was passing across the stall—a lot of money—far too much, but she knew instinctively that if she even so much as hinted that he was being extravagant, he would be annoyed. All the same, the money would have bought warm socks for the children...

Evidently that point of view hadn't occurred to her companion; he appeared quite unworried at his expenditure, took her arm again and strolled on until they reached the end of the canal, where he turned down a narrow street which led them to Oude Delft. 'Tea?' he enquired. 'I live close by and the children are always famished when they get home.'

She wondered just where close by was. The houses on either side of the canal were large; museums, converted offices, large family mansions for those who could still afford to maintain them. She didn't have to wonder for long; he crossed one of the little arched bridges and paused before the massive door of a patrician house, its flat-faced front ornamented in the rococo style with a great deal of plaster work.

'Here?' asked Constantia in an unbelieving voice.

Her companion had taken out a key and turned to look at her. 'Er—yes.'

'You live here? I thought…oh, it's a flat.'

'No, it's a house—the owner allows me to live in it.'

'How kind of him—a relation, I expect.' She skipped past him into the hall, quite happy again. For one moment she had wondered if he was actually the owner of all this magnificence. For it was magnificent; a vast square hall, its white marble floor covered with thin silk rugs, an elaborately carved staircase rising grandly from its centre, and the sort of furniture that one saw in museums—only the atmosphere wasn't like a museum at all. The house was lived in and cared for. She wondered who coped with the vast amount of polishing and cleaning evident in the hall alone. 'Do you have a daily woman?' she asked.

The doctor looked surprised and then amused, but he answered carefully: 'Oh, yes, a very good woman, her name's Rietje. She's not here this afternoon, though. I expect the children will get the tea; they'll be here at any moment.' He shut the massive door behind him. 'Ah, here are Solly and Sheba and Prince. There's a cat in the kitchen—the children, you know,' he added vaguely.

Constantia nodded her understanding. 'Of course, they have to have pets.'

She stood a little irresolutely, for her host appeared lost in thought—or was he listening for something? She decided that she was mistaken, for he spoke to the dogs and then said: 'Do take your coat off,' and took it from her and tossed it on to one of the carved chairs against one wall, then tossed his on top of it. 'Shall we go into the sitting room?'

It was a grand room, grandly furnished with rich brocade curtains at its windows and more fine rugs on the polished wood floor, but somehow it was comfortable too, with great armchairs and sofas of an inviting softness, and delicate little tables. There were bookshelves too and a pile of children's comics and a half-finished game of Monopoly. Constantia drew an admiring breath.

'It's beautiful,' she exclaimed, 'and so exquisitely furnished. Doesn't the owner mind you being here?' An expression she couldn't read crossed her companion's face and she hastened to add: 'I didn't mean you—I was thinking of the children. Three of them, you know, however good they are—I mean, breaking things and finger marks…'

The expression had gone, if ever she had seen it. He said easily, 'He doesn't object—he likes children, you see. Besides, he understands that they're well behaved and wouldn't break or spoil anything if they could help it. There's a big room upstairs which they use as a playroom, and he doesn't mind how much that gets battered.'

Her voice was warm. 'He must be a nice man.' She looked around her again. 'You'd think that he would want to live here himself.'

'He likes the country.'

'Oh, yes, I suppose he would if he's elderly. He must have a great deal of money if he has two houses. Is he married?'

She had crossed the room to look at a flower painting and had her back to the doctor, who had bent to tickle Prince's ears. 'No—he's rather a lonely man.'

Her pretty face was full of sympathy as she turned to face him. 'Oh, the poor dear—if only he had a wife and children—being lonely is terrible.'

Her companion echoed her. 'Terrible, and if only he had…'

'Anyway, he must be a perfect dear to allow you all to live here, though I expect he feels that this house was built for a family. Your…uncle?' She paused and looked enquiringly at the doctor. 'He is a relation?'

He nodded. 'Oh, certainly of my blood.'

'Yes, well—I daresay he loves this place very much and likes to know that there are children in it.'

'I'm sure that he does—here they come now. They use the little door in the garden wall at the back.'

They surged in, all talking at once, laughing and calling to each other, running to greet the doctor and then Constantia, delighted to see her again. The doctor prised them loose, quite unperturbed by the din going on around him, and said firmly in English: 'Wash your hands for tea, my dears—it's in the kitchen.'

Pieter and Paul exchanged glances and looked mischievous, and Elisabeth burst into a torrent of Dutch. Constantia had no idea what the doctor said to them, only that they chorused, '*Ja*, Oom Jeroen,' and flew from the room; she could hear them giggling together as they crossed the hall and the doctor said easily: 'Don't mind the mirth—speaking English always sends them into paroxysms.'

Constantia giggled too. 'You've got your hands full, haven't you? But they're pretty super, aren't they?'

In her room that evening, getting ready for bed, she allowed her thoughts to linger over the day while her eyes dwelt on the flowers arranged in the variety of vases and jars she had managed to collect around the house. It had been tremendous fun and much, much nicer than she had ever supposed it would be. The market had been great, but tea with the

doctor and his small relatives had been marvellous. They had sat at the big scrubbed table
in the centre of the enormous kitchen, with its
windows overlooking the garden at the back of
the house, and eaten the sort of tea she remembered from her own childhood. Bread and butter and jam and a large cake to cut at, and
when she had remarked upon it the doctor had
assured her that although it certainly wasn't the
rule in Holland, where a small cup of milkless
tea and a biscuit or a chocolate were considered quite sufficient, he had found that the children, hungry from school, enjoyed a more sub-
stantial meal when they got home and then
only needed a light supper at bedtime.

And after tea they had all washed up and
gone back upstairs to play Monopoly until
bedtime, when she had helped Elisabeth get
ready for bed, and when she had gone downstairs again there had been her host with a coffee tray on the table before the great fireplace
in the sitting room. There had been little
chicken patties and sausage rolls too, and when
she asked who did the cooking, it was to hear
that Rietje did that too, and from time to time

produced the dainties they were eating for their supper.

All the same, thought Constantia worriedly as she sat on the edge of her bed, giving her soft fine hair its regulation one hundred strokes, Doctor van der Giessen must have his work cut out. She got into bed, her mind busy—longing to know more about him.

Mrs Dowling had said that he was poor, and that didn't matter at all to Constantia; she would have liked to know more about him as a person. Did he have a large practice, she wondered, and was his sister his only relation other than the children? And surely there must be a girl somewhere in his life? She curled up in bed, trying to imagine what she would be like—a very special girl; the doctor deserved that. He was just about the nicest man she had ever met. She wondered how old he was, too. Perhaps, if they saw each other fairly frequently while she was in Delft, she could ask him. She began to worry as to how much longer she would be there; Mrs Dowling wasn't quite like her other cases, who, sooner or later, had got well enough for her to leave them. Mrs Dowling didn't really need a nurse at all, and if she had been sensible she could have learned to give herself her insulin injections and cope with her own diet. Constantia found herself hoping that she would be needed for some time yet; true, it was boring with no actual nursing to do, and Mrs Dowling was just about the most tiresome patient she had ever encountered.

And as if to emphasise that opinion, Mrs Dowling was worse than ever the next morning. Her breakfast was uneatable; Constantia had hurt her when she had given her injection; an old friend who was a cornerstone of her bridge table had gone to England and left her with a choice of most inferior substitutes. And the wrong newspaper had been delivered.

Constantia, busy charting insulin doses and sugar levels, was told to leave what she was doing and fetch the correct one, 'and at the same time you might as well go into that needlework shop in Gerritstraat and see if that embroidery silk I ordered has arrived.' She added crossly: 'And go now.'

Constantia went, glad to escape and glad to have the opportunity of telephoning Doctor Sperling to let him know that Mrs Dowling's tests were all over the place again. Either she was hopelessly unstabilised, which in view of the doctor's treatment was absurd, or she was eating something she shouldn't be.

There was a telephone in the hotel close by, so she left a message with the doctor's secretary and went on her way to the newsagent. She had collected the newspaper and the embroidery silk and was on her way back through the shopping precinct when Doctor van der Giessen came out of the same door as he had done before.

'Playing truant?' he wanted to know.

She laughed. 'No; changing the newspaper and fetching something Mrs Dowling ordered.'

He fell into step beside her. 'Why can't she do these things for herself?' he enquired mildly.

'Well—I'm not sure…' She hesitated. 'Is it all right if I tell you something, or isn't it ethical?'

He smiled down at her. 'I don't suppose it would matter—Doctor Sperling and I have known each other for quite some time. What seems to be the matter?'

'I left a message with Doctor Sperling's secretary. Mrs Dowling isn't stabilising and she ought to be.'

'Ah—the odd hunk of cheese or bar of chocolate?' he commented placidly. 'I shouldn't be at all surprised—a few days in hospital would see to that. I expect Doctor Sperling will have that at the back of his mind.' They were crossing the bridge and weren't hurrying in the sunshine. 'The children want to know when you're coming to tea again.'

'Oh, do they? How sweet of them.'

'On your next half day, perhaps?'

'I'd like that very much—about four o'clock? It will be Wednesday.'

'I've a surgery until three-thirty, come then—if no one answers the door walk in and make yourself at home.'

'I could get the tea if you wouldn't mind me going to the kitchen,' Constantia offered.

'Splendid.' They had come to a halt in front of the hotel again.

'I must go,' she said regretfully.

'*Tot ziens*, then.'

She watched him disappear down a small street in the direction of Oude Delft and then went slowly on her way. Life was really rather pleasant, she decided as she waited for Nel to open the door.

It wasn't quite as pleasant as she went into Mrs Dowling's room.

'There you are!' Her patient's harsh voice was pitched high with impatience; she scarcely glanced up from manicuring her nails. 'You've been a long time.'

'Not quite half an hour,' said Constantia quietly. She put the newspaper and the silk on a table with the little pile of change, which Mrs Dowling leaned over and counted carefully before telling Constantia to give her her handbag. 'Did you meet someone?' she demanded.

'Doctor van der Giessen.'

Mrs Dowling closed her handbag with a snap. 'Him?' Her lip curled in a sneer. 'Sweet on him, are you? I told you that he was as poor as a church mouse—so rumour says—and likely to stay that way, with three children to look after. More fool he!'

Constantia was collecting the odds and ends Mrs Dowling had shed around the room. The remark ruffled her patience and her temper, but she had no intention of letting her patient see that. 'Probably he prefers children to money,' she commented lightly, 'some people do.'

Mrs Dowling shot her a peevish look. 'That's ridiculous, and you're being impertinent, Nurse.'

Constantia let that pass. 'Would you like cheese or ham with your salad?' she wanted to know.

'Neither. You can think up something else; that's what I pay you for, isn't it? I'm tired of this dreary diet. I'm sure Doctor Sperling has exaggerated the whole business—I'll have escalope of veal with a cream sauce.'

'Followed by a diabetic coma,' Constantia added silently while she observed out loud, 'I'm afraid a diet is necessary, Mrs Dowling. Once you're stabilised Doctor Sperling will allow you more variety. I'll go and see about your lunch and then give you your injection.'

She was almost at the door when Mrs Dowling called after her in her penetrating voice: 'Are you going to ask for time off to meet your doctor? I daresay he could afford a cup of coffee somewhere.'

Constantia fought and conquered a desire to throw something at her patient and went out of the room without saying a word, although she muttered nastily to herself on her way to the kitchen.

Wednesday came; Constantia bounced out of bed, observed that it was a lovely morning, even if cold still, and set about dealing with her patient's wants. It was almost lunchtime when the doorbell rang and a visitor was shown in by Nel—a young man with rather vapid good looks, who embraced Mrs Dowling with every appearance of delight and addressed her as Vera.

'My nephew, Willy Caxton—passing through Delft and lunching with us,' explained Mrs Dowling briefly. She nodded at Constantia. 'My nurse.'

They exchanged a cool greeting because Constantia was smarting under the assumption that she had no name and he obviously didn't consider it worth his while to ask. 'Give Mr Caxton a drink,' decreed Mrs Dowling, 'and then go and see about lunch. Nel should have it ready.'

It was almost one o'clock. Constantia, hurrying a Nel who didn't want to be hurried, found herself fretting and fuming that she wouldn't be able to escape for her half day. Luckily she wasn't expected until half past three...

It was during lunch that Mrs Dowling told Constantia that she was to escort her nephew to as many of the local places of interest as could be squashed into a couple of hours.

'It's my half day, Mrs Dowling, and I've already made other arrangements.'

'Nonsense, what arrangements could you possibly have?' Her employer's eyes narrowed. 'Going out with your doctor, I suppose? Well, he'll just have to wait, won't he? Mr Caxton will be leaving at four o'clock, you can have the rest of the day to yourself.'

Constantia was on the point of refusing
point blank; it was Willy's rather plaintive re-
quest to agree to his aunt's wishes which
melted her too-soft heart. He was so obviously
anxious to get away as soon as possible. 'Until
half past three?' she conceded, and went to get
her outdoor things.

He was hard going; not in the least interested in the town or its lovely buildings. Indeed, he confided in Constantia, if it wasn't
that Aunt Vera had left him a tidy little sum
in her will, he wouldn't bother to come and
see her at all. Constantia liked him even less
for saying that; his good looks were skin-deep
and she had the strong impression that the only
thing that mattered to him was himself and his
own doings. She rushed him from one church
to the next, pointed out some of the more beautiful buildings, knowing that he wasn't in the
least interested, and wanted to know, with
some asperity, if he wouldn't like to cut short
his sightseeing. It was already well past half
past three—she would never get to Doctor van
der Giessen's house in time now.

They were standing on the edge of the Markt where he had parked his car, while she urged him to get in and drive away as nicely as she could without actually giving him a push, when Doctor van der Giessen's battered Fiat drove slowly by. He saw them but he didn't stop, only gave her an expressionless look which held no hint of an invitation to tea.

It was a pity that Willy Caxton chose that moment to catch her by the hand and look earnestly into her face. He was only begging her to assure his aunt that he had had a delightful afternoon and to refrain from mentioning that he was leaving before he was supposed to, but she could hardly stop the doctor's car to tell him that.

She gave Willy only half her attention as she watched the Fiat rush round a corner and out of sight. She wouldn't dare to go to tea now; she had wasted almost half an hour getting the wretched Willy to go, and probably the doctor thought that she had stood his tea party up for the pleasures of Willy's tiresome company.

Her half day was spoiled; she waved Willy a thankful goodbye and wandered away, wondering if she should telephone the doctor's house or even go there. But in the face of that bland look she had received from the car she didn't dare. She would write a little note. She had tea in the little tea shop by the market, composing it in her head while she did so. She went for a long walk afterwards, eating her supper in a snack bar and then walking again. The half day she had so looked forward to had been a washout.

# CHAPTER THREE

IT WAS the following afternoon as she was returning from her few hours off duty that Constantia encountered Elisabeth. The child was crying, and so upset that Constantia had to remind her who she was before she would stop sobbing to say:

'We've lost Prince—Pieter and Paul are looking for him too—we aren't supposed to be out, but we left the garden door open when we got home and he ran out. We didn't find out at first, and when we went to look for him he'd gone.' She burst into fresh sobs and Constantia stooped to wipe the woebegone little face and say comfortingly: 'He can't be far, poppet, and he knows his way home, doesn't he?'

'We've only had him a week or two—Oom Jeroen found him in a ditch and brought him home to live with us.' The little girl raised her tear-stained face to hers and Constantia said cheerfully, 'Look, darling, you go home—

carefully, mind, and I'll start looking for Prince. Will you do that and wait until I come? Promise?'

The moppet nodded and Constantia took her across the narrow street and saw her safely on her way before starting her search for the little dog. She found him within ten minutes, lying in a gutter of one of the side streets she had been methodically combing. He was lying very still, but when she ran to him he wagged his ridiculous tail. There was a spot of blood on his nose and a long wound along his ribs, but his eyes were bright.

'I'll have you home in a brace of shakes,' Constantia promised him, 'but I'm going to have to hurt you, my boy, so grit your teeth.'

She scooped him up into her arms in one gentle movement and although he bared the teeth she had urged him to grit, he didn't bite her, only whimpered.

The doctor's house was close by; just at the bottom of the lane and then round the corner and across the canal. She walked as quickly as she dared, telling Prince to be a good boy as she went. There was no one to be seen, but

once in Oude Delft she sighted Pieter and Paul
hurrying along, going away from her. Her
shrill whistle turned their heads and they came
running back to fetch up beside her, their anxious eyes on Prince.

'He's hurt,' she told them in a reassuring
voice, 'but I don't think it's too bad. Pieter,
run on and open the door, we'll take him
straight to the kitchen. And get a blanket or
something to put on the table.'

Elisabeth was at the door when Constantia
reached it and broke at once into a babble of
Dutch, tears still streaming down her small
cheeks. 'Now, now,' said Constantia, 'don't
cry, poppet—get me a towel and a bowl and
some water from the tap—they'll all be in the
kitchen. Paul, where's your uncle?'

'He had to go out to a case in one of the
villages. Is Prince very ill, Miss Morley?'

'Call me Constantia, dear. I don't know. We
must clean him up gently, and your uncle will
have a look when he gets here.' She had
reached the kitchen by now and had laid Prince
down on the folded blanket. He wagged his tail
as she slipped his collar off and began, very

gingerly, to clean up the wound in his side. It was ugly enough but not, she thought, dangerously so, but there could be other injuries. The children stood round in a hushed circle, scarcely breathing, so intent on what she was doing that none of them heard the doctor's quiet approach. The moment they did however, they all began to explain at once.

'One at a time,' he said calmly, and as Constantia stood back, bent over Prince. Paul's tale was interrupted a dozen times by the others and by the time he had finished, his uncle had examined the dog, taking no notice of its lifted lip, talking to it quietly as he poked and prodded with large, gentle fingers.

'A couple of ribs,' he pronounced, 'and a nasty cut here—there's another one on his muzzle. I'll get the vet and we'll have him all right in no time.'

Constantia heard the sighs of relief from the children, unaware that she had sighed too. She felt a warm tongue on her hand and looked down to find Sheba and Solly standing beside her, and said: 'Oh, they're here too.'

The doctor turned to look at her, then: 'They were with me,' he told her. 'Thank you for finding Prince and bringing him home—we're all very grateful.' His voice was pleasant, but he didn't smile and she found herself stammering a little: 'I do hope he's not badly hurt—I'm glad that I...'

He had turned away to bend over Prince again and none of the children answered her, indeed they didn't look up, either. Constantia waited a moment and then went quietly from the kitchen and across the hall to the still open front door, shutting it silently behind her, and reflected as she did so that she was shutting herself out, but that the doctor had, metaphorically speaking, already done that.

She went quickly down Oude Delft and up a side street into the Wijnhaven and so presently to Mrs Dowling's house. She would be late, but there was nothing to be done about that now.

Mrs Dowling was in a mood. 'You're late. Why?'

Constantia took time to answer her. 'Only a few minutes, Mrs Dowling, and I was half an hour late going off duty.'

'Impertinence!' Her patient gobbled with bad temper. 'But it's just as well you're back. I've eaten some chocolates. I sent Nel out for some—delicious ones with soft caramel centres.' She nodded carelessly towards a box lying on the floor beside her chaise-lounge. 'They're there.'

'How long ago did you eat them?' asked Constantia calmly.

Mrs Dowling shrugged. 'My dear nurse, how should I know? An hour—half an hour.'

'Then we shall have to wait a little while and see how you feel, Mrs Dowling.'

Her patient sat up with no trace of her usual languid movements. 'I may go into a coma.'

'Quite likely, but I shall be watching for the first symptoms and we can prevent that happening. In the meantime, I'll ring Doctor Sperling.'

The doctor wasn't home. The voice at the other end of the telephone repeated: *'Niet thuis,'* several times, and Constantia sighed as she went back to her patient. She wasn't quite sure that Mrs Dowling was telling the truth; she was a devious woman and spoilt. She was bored too, and boredom caused people to do strange things. All the same she played safe, setting out syringe, glucose and insulin ready for immediate use, and then spent the next ten minutes coaxing Mrs Dowling to provide her with a specimen.

Constantia hadn't been a Ward Sister for nothing; her patient was overbearing and intent on making life hard for those around her, but she was her patient, and personal feelings didn't come into it. All the same, it took all her patience and tact to get what she wanted, but it was worth the effort. Mrs Dowling was loaded with sugar.

Constantia, tidying the room, took the opportunity to peep into the chocolate box; it was half empty. She picked it up without comment and put it away in a cupboard, all the while talking pleasantly about nothing much while her mind was busy working out calories and units of insulin. Mrs Dowling was sulking now and frightened, which had the effect of making her even more unpleasant than usual.

Neither of them heard the doorbell. Nel opened the door with something of a flourish and ushered in Doctor van der Giessen. His good evening was nicely professional and he added: 'Doctor Sperling's wife telephoned me; he asked me to cover for him if he shouldn't be available. What's the trouble?' He addressed himself to Constantia, and although his manner was pleasant enough she could sense his reserve.

'Mrs Dowling has eaten some chocolates. I don't know exactly how many—about three or four ounces, I should suppose. There's an orange reaction and ketones—I thought that Doctor Sperling should be told.'

'Quite right, Nurse. Pulse? Nausea, vomiting?'

'Nausea, nothing else.'

'In that case, perhaps I might take a look at your tongue, Mrs Dowling?'

He examined her carefully, cheerfully ignoring her peevish demands for Doctor Sperling, and when he had finished he wrote up her chart and handed it to Constantia. 'That should take care of everything, I fancy. Give the insulin straight away, will you? And a further dose after two hours, according to the sugar level.' He went to his bag and took out a syringe and a small glass tube which Constantia took from him. Mrs Dowling moaned and cried and he soothed her like a small child as he took the blood he needed for a blood sugar test, assured her that she would be quite all right in no time at all, and prepared to leave.

'You can't leave me, I'm in danger,' declared Mrs Dowling.

'Not any more, Mrs Dowling, and Nurse Morley knows exactly what to do.'

'I insist on you staying!'

'I'm taking evening surgery,' he explained mildly. 'If you were in the least danger, I would remain. If Nurse Morley is worried she can contact me at once.' He said good evening in a calm unhurried manner and went to the door, saying to Constantia as he went: 'Let me know the result of the tests as you do them, will you? Supper as I suggest on the chart— the insulin is adjusted. Doctor Sperling won't be back until very late, but I'll give him the facts.'

He nodded to her and she was again aware of reserve in his manner. Dealing gently with the tiresome Mrs Dowling, she thought sadly of a friendship which had somehow died.

By bedtime, Mrs Dowling was normal again; for once quite subdued, she had submitted to injections, tests and eaten every crumb of the supper prescribed for her. She even went to bed without fuss, leaving Constantia to fetch her supper and go thankfully to her own room.

She was crossing the hall, balancing her tray, when the doorbell pinged once and she went to answer it. Doctor van der Giessen was on the step, looking vast and placid. He came into the hall, closed the door behind him and asked: 'Crisis over, I take it?'

'Yes, thank you.'

His gaze lighted on the tray. 'Supper?' he wanted to know.

'Yes. Mrs Dowling is in bed, quite worn out but otherwise just as she should be. Did you want to see her?'

He shook his head. 'No need. I came to see you.'

'Me?'

'My thanks were inadequate on Prince's behalf. You were kind, sensible and gentle, and we let you leave the house without so much as a word.'

She smiled rather shyly. 'It's quite all right. He needed all the attention he could get, didn't he? Is he all right?'

'He'll do. The vet has patched him up and he's lying with Solly and Sheba on each side of him and the cat playing mother.' His eyes searched her face. 'You didn't come to tea.'

She was so glad that she could explain now, that the words came tumbling out of her mouth in a bit of a muddle. 'You see, I didn't like to come because I was late—I was going to post a letter this afternoon, explaining...'

'Why were you late?'

'Mrs Dowling's nephew came to lunch and she insisted that I should show him as much of Delft as possible. I told her that I had my afternoon planned, but she wouldn't listen, and Willy Caxton—' she paused to chuckle, 'isn't that a simply super name?—was too scared of her to do anything but agree. He was supposed to stay until four o'clock because she said so, but I persuaded him to go sooner; all the same it was well past that time when he actually went.' She gave him a candid look. 'If you hadn't driven past I would have walked round to your house and explained, but you looked cross—no, not quite that, put out.'

'I expect I was disappointed.' He was smiling down at her.

'Were you? I know I was. It's not nice to lose a friend.'

He went over to the tray and poured out a cup of coffee, and came back with it to put it into her hand and press her gently into a rather uncomfortable little chair. 'Your supper's spoiling. You've not lost a friend, Constantia. I think we're going to be friends for the rest of our lives.'

She sipped the tepid drink. 'That's nice. Even if you don't see friends—and we're not likely to see each other once I've left here, are we?—it's nice to know they're only a letter away.'

'You don't expect to stay here long?' He was at the tray again, inspecting the macaroni cheese with a disdainful lift of his high-bridged nose.

'Well, I shouldn't think so. I don't have much to do now.' She accepted her supper, wrinkled her pretty nose at it and put it down. 'I don't think I'm hungry.'

There was no expression on her companion's face. 'I hope you will give us all the pleasure of having supper with us on your next free half day off.' He had buttered the roll on her tray and handed it to her. 'Eat that. Let me see—when will that be?'

She bit into the bread, and with her mouth full, told him: 'Well, Mrs Dowling did say Sunday, but perhaps she might change her mind.'

'Let us hope that she won't. Shall we take everyone for a walk first? Then tea and one of those noisy games I seem to get embroiled in from time to time…I'll get Rietje to cook us a nice supper.'

Constantia put out her tongue to catch a crumb on her cheek. 'That sounds lovely.' She smiled warmly at him. 'You're very kind.'

He said gravely: 'You don't find our company tedious? We lead a very quiet life.'

'One never leads a quiet life with children,' she pointed out.

'I was really referring to the bright lights, theatres and dinner out and people in for drinks.' His eyes were very sharp on her face, but she wasn't looking at him.

'I've never had a chance to live like that,' she told him. 'I expect it's great fun if you're with the right person.'

He filled her cup with the now cold coffee and she drank it absentmindedly. He said casually: 'You mean if one were married to the right person? Certainly it would be fun to share one's pleasures.'

'But have a home life too,' she interpolated anxiously.

'Naturally.'

'But then the bright lights wouldn't matter, would they? Nice to have, but not essential.'

'Pretty clothes, jewellery?'

'Thrown in as a bonus?' she laughed up at him. 'Lovely, but not if they were to turn me into someone like Mrs Dowling.'

He eyed her in a leisurely fashion and said slowly: 'I don't think you could look or be like her in a thousand years.'

She got to her feet. 'There speaks a true friend. Do you really not want to see her? She's asleep, but I don't think you would disturb her.'

'I really don't want to see her. I must go home—I've been to see a patient and it seemed sensible to call in.'

'Thank you. Will Doctor Sperling be along tomorrow?'

He nodded. 'I've told him not an hour since. He'll be round after surgery, but don't hesitate to telephone if you're worried.'

She saw him to the door and stood on the step, watching him walk away. He was a kind and good man, she thought, and so easy to talk to, and she did enjoy his company. He was like an elder brother—well, perhaps not quite, but an old family friend, someone she had known all her life.

Mrs Dowling made herself unpleasant for the next day or two; it was as though she blamed Constantia for her regrettable inroads into the forbidden chocolates. But Constantia, anticipating the pleasures of her half day, bore her ill-humour with fortitude, obeyed Doctor Sperling's instructions to the letter, and kept an unobtrusive but eagle eye on her patient's activities. Not that Mrs Dowling had many; she dressed for the day, fussing over her face and her hair and her nails, received her friends and played her eternal bridge—and any time there was over she filled in nicely with complaints. She had made one or two snide remarks about Constantia's free time, but Constantia refused to be drawn; her free time was her own and she kept discreetly quiet about it.

It was raining on Sunday when she got up. It continued to rain throughout the morning and Constantia was on edge throughout lunch, expecting Mrs Dowling to tell her that she might as well have her half day at some other time so that she could go out. But fortunately she was too occupied in deciding whom she should invite to a small evening party she intended giving, and Constantia, clad in a sensible raincoat and with a scarf over her hair, made her escape.

The weather, it seemed, made no difference to the doctor and his small relations; the party set out for the promised walk, suitably clad and apparently not caring about rain and wind. The dogs came too, Sheba and Solly at their master's heels, and Prince, looking quite ridiculous with his head poked through a hole in a plastic cape, cradled in the doctor's arms. 'Couldn't leave him alone,' he pointed out, 'and there's a quiet patch of grass where he can walk around for a minute or two.'

The children and the Alsatians skipped and ran around them while the doctor and Constantia walked more soberly, Prince walking gingerly beside them before being returned to the crook of the doctor's vast arm. And all the while they talked; trying to remember later, Constantia had difficulty in remembering exactly what they had talked about. Nothing much, she supposed. All the same, when they turned for home she was surprised to find that the afternoon was rapidly sliding into dusk.

They had tea in the kitchen again, a generous spread to which they all did full justice, with Constantia wielding the teapot while they worked their way through sandwiches and cake and *ontbijtkeok* and *appel gebak*. They played Monopoly again when they had washed up, sitting on the splendid rugs in the sitting room, and Constantia, quite carried away at winning mythical thousands and then losing it all again, made just as much noise as the children. And presently she went to the kitchen, where she felt quite at home by now, and made cocoa for the children before they went to their beds.

They slept on the second floor, in what was obviously the nursery wing, with a playroom from which a number of bedrooms led. It was all very cosy and as Elisabeth assured her, they could summon their uncle at once by the house telephone in the boys' room. Constantia wondered uneasily what happened when the doctor had to go out at night—did he leave the children alone?—perhaps Rietje slept in when he was on call for the hospital or expected a night case.

She broached the subject when she went back downstairs and the doctor, after only the tiniest pause, said easily: 'Oh, Rietje is very good about sleeping here,' and went on to tell her about an interesting case he had had during the week, so that she dismissed the matter without another thought.

The unseen Rietje had certainly done them proud for their supper. Constantia, accompanying the doctor down to the kitchen, laid the table while he fetched the food. There was soup ready on the stove and a mouth-watering *quiche* in the oven, and asparagus and potato straws, as well as a fresh fruit salad and cream for afters.

'Whenever did she do all this?' asked Constantia, 'and how did she manage to keep it just exactly right for us to eat?'

'It was no trouble to warm up while you were upstairs with Elisabeth,' he told her placidly. 'Would you like a sherry first?'

The kitchen was warm; its dark oak fitments reflecting the flames in the opened front of the Aga stove. The doctor had produced a bottle of Liebfraumilch to go with the food, and Con-

stantia, inured to Mrs Dowling's somewhat re-
stricted diet, enjoyed herself. They didn't
hurry, there was no need, but talked as they
ate although the doctor hadn't much to tell her
about himself; indeed, by the end of the meal
she came to the conclusion that she knew no
more about him than on the day they had met.
She was on the point of saying so when the
telephone rang and in answer to her questioning look, he said: 'I switched it through when
we came downstairs—you'll excuse me?'

He went over to where it hung on the wall
and stood listening, frowning a little, and presently began to speak to someone on the other
end. He sounded brisk and very sure of himself, and Constantia wondered just what post
he held at the hospital—something senior, she
felt, judging from the assurance in his voice.

He rang off presently and came back to the
table, saying pleasantly, 'One of my cases in
hospital—not desperate, though.'

All the same she said instantly, 'You want
to go—I'll go back to Mrs Dowling.' She was
actually out of her chair when he pushed her
gently back into it.

'What a splendid girl you are—not so much as a pout or frown. Yes, I'll have to go, but I shan't be gone long. Would you stay here— the children, you know—' and when she nodded, 'we can have coffee when I get back. Go and curl up by the sitting room fire.' He smiled. 'I'll telephone if anything turns up.' He had gone without fuss; the door shut quietly behind him.

Constantia washed up then and left the kitchen tidy, and laid the breakfast table. The coffee tray had been left ready and the coffee was on the Aga. She paused to admire the massive silver coffee pot on the tray and the matching cream jug and sugar bowl; they were old and beautifully polished, and she wondered again who found the time to keep everything so exquisitely. Presently she wandered upstairs and sat down before the fire, a magazine open beside her, not reading it. She wondered if the doctor had lived in the house for a long time; perhaps it had been lent to him for the rest of his life, or perhaps he would inherit it from the old relation who owned it. She was ruminating over these possibilities when he returned, coming unhurriedly into the room.

'Don't get up,' he told her, 'I'll fetch the coffee. Have the children been all right?'

'I crept up to see—they're all asleep. Was everything OK at the hospital?'

He nodded. 'Yes—I've an excellent Registrar.' He saw her surprise. 'I have a few beds there—nothing like as many as Doctor Sperling.'

He went away and came back almost immediately with the coffee and set it on a little table near the fire, and then went to sit in his great winged chair on the other side of the hearth. Constantia felt that she had never been so content, but presently, and with reluctance, she told him that she must go back, and despite her protestations he went with her. The children would be all right for ten minutes, he assured her, and besides, he had warned Pieter that he would be taking her home some time during the evening.

They walked quickly through the quiet streets, too short a walk, thought Constantia, chattering away happily, telling her companion how much she had enjoyed her walk and the lovely supper and pausing in this to beg him to observe what a lovely night it was after the rain. The doctor strode along beside her, not saying much, but somehow that didn't seem to matter; she could feel his friendliness although they were walking apart.

Nel had lent her a latchkey and he took it from her to open the street door and then put it back into her hand But he didn't let her hand go, he held it fast in his own large one so that she looked up at him enquiringly. 'I'm glad you liked being with us, Constantia. We—I liked having you. Will you come again? When do you have your next half day?'

'I don't know... Mrs Dowling doesn't always tell me.'

'Then I'll telephone each day until she does.' He smiled at her and then bent and kissed her gently on her cheek. 'Goodnight,' he said, and opened the door for her.

The kiss had surprised her, but of course everybody kissed these days, she told herself as she trod softly up to her room. She was undressed and in her dressing gown when she remembered that she had to take the key back to Nel who, when Constantia had her half days, was supposed to stay awake until she got in. The maid was already asleep, so Constantia laid the key on the bedside table and crept down to Mrs Dowling's room and peeped round the half open door. Her patient was sleeping a nice healthy sleep; she sighed with relief and went at last to her own bed.

Doctor van der Giessen telephoned just as he said he would, and as luck would have it it was Mrs Dowling who answered it, for the telephone was by her chair so that she could use it without bothering to move out of it. Constantia, in the kitchen frowning over calories for lunch, heard her patient's strident voice and belted upstairs, her mind already dealing with the treatment of insulin comas, to be met with Mrs Dowling's mocking: 'Your boy-friend, Nurse—and you can tell him from me that he can stop telephoning you at my house.'

Constantia didn't answer but picked up the receiver, and Doctor van der Giessen's placid voice observed: 'I've set the cat among the pigeons, haven't I? When is your half day?'

'I don't know.' She was very conscious of Mrs Dowling's beady eye on her back.

'Then ask—now.' The voice was still placid, but it obviously expected obedience.

So Constantia turned round and asked and Mrs Dowling said nastily: 'Why do you want to know?'

'I should like to make some arrangements of my own, Mrs Dowling.'

'I haven't decided.'

Constantia's patience was wearing thin—she wasn't quick-tempered, but now she felt rage boiling around inside her. 'I must remind you that I am entitled to two full days off a week, Mrs Dowling. Because of your dislike of being left alone until you were stabilised, I've not insisted on them. I think that I have every right to know on which days I may have my quite inadequate half days.'

Mrs Dowling's eyes glittered with temper. Constantia watched her struggling to suppress it and waited calmly.

'Well,' burst out that lady finally, 'I've never heard anything like it!' She caught Constantia's eyes fixed on her and ended lamely: 'Oh, well, have it your own way. You can have Tuesday.'

'And the second half day?' prompted Constantia.

'Saturday, I suppose.' She glared furiously. 'You wait…' she began, but Constantia wasn't listening. She was saying happily into the receiver: 'Tuesday and Saturday.'

'Good. I've visits on Tuesday, but there's no reason why you shouldn't come with me in the car, is there? We'll be back in time to give the children their tea.'

Mrs Dowling had a good deal to say about it, of course; little spiteful remarks about doctors and nurses and girls on their own making the most of their chances, but Constantia didn't listen. It wasn't like that at all; Mrs Dowling had got it all wrong. There was such a thing as friendship and there was nothing cheap about that.

On Tuesday, sitting beside the doctor in his car, she told Doctor van der Giessen all about it. 'I'm sorry for the poor soul,' declared Constantia, 'she hasn't any friends—not like you and me, I mean. Only people who come and play bridge and talk about each other behind their backs.'

The doctor agreed gravely, his eyes on the road ahead of him. 'And have you many friends in England, Constantia?' he wanted to know.

She thought about it before she answered. 'Oh, yes, but I don't think I could ask any of them to do something without even bothering to think if they would.' She frowned because she hadn't put it very well. 'Do you see?' she added.

'I see. I hope you haven't added me to their numbers? I can promise you that I would— er—do anything you asked without thinking it over first.'

'So would I do that for you. Have you a great many friends?'

They were out of the town now, and he turned off the road to drive down a narrow side road between fields. 'Yes, but I have a large family, you see, and one meets a lot of people…'

She was rather taken aback. 'Oh—I didn't know. I suppose I thought that you had a sister and that was all.'

'My parents are dead, but I have another sister and two brothers, and more cousins and aunts and uncles than I care to remember.'

She said in a sad little voice before she could stop herself: 'So you don't really need any more friends.'

He stopped the car with smooth suddenness. 'Constantia, my family are scattered and there isn't a friend among my many friends who could fill your place.'

She said with a sudden burst of candour: 'Mrs Dowling said I was out to get you, but I'm not. She's a vulgar woman.' She looked at him as she spoke, determined to be quite honest.

His face was as placid as always, only he was smiling a little. 'Very vulgar,' he conceded, 'and I have never for one moment imagined that you were—er—out to get me.' He looked away for a moment. 'I'm surprised at her; did she not warn you that I had no money?'

'Oh, days ago. As though that matters—I don't think I'd want to be friends with some-one rich. They might think you were making up to them all the time and you'd never be quite sure, would you?'

'Probably not. I must say you have it in for the rich, haven't you?'

He was smiling again and Constantia smiled back. 'Only people like Mrs Dowling. I expect there are a lot of nice rich people about, only one doesn't meet them.'

He started the car again. 'Perhaps because the nice ones don't find it important enough to talk about.'

His voice was silky; she looked at him in surprise. 'You sound cross—have I said something to vex you?'

They were making good headway on the brick surface of the road. 'Constantia, I don't think that you could vex me. But believe me, there are some very worthwhile people around with money, who use it wisely even though it's more than they need.'

'Poor things!' She spoke with heartfelt sympathy. 'Though I expect if they're as nice as you say they put it to very good use.' They had turned in through an open gate into a farmyard. 'Is this where you have a patient?'

'Two—measles.'

The afternoon passed swiftly; the visits were for the most part to outlying farms, giving ample opportunity for conversation, and when they got back to the house in Oude Delft the children joined them within a few minutes and the pleasant pattern of tea and card games and bed wove itself into the rest of the day. True, the doctor had surgery after tea, but by the time Constantia and the children had washed up the tea-things and gone to the sitting room for a game of cards, he was able to join them for a rowdy game of Scrabble, played in Dutch for Constantia's benefit. They had supper together when the children had gone to bed and he took her back to Mrs Dowling's afterwards, only this time he didn't kiss her.

Saturday was much the same, only the doctor had no surgery in the evening; they went for a walk in the afternoon and the invisible

Rietje had done them proud with cake and sandwiches for tea. They sat round the kitchen table, all talking at once, with the dogs joining in and the cat sitting on Constantia's lap. Just as home should be, she thought contentedly. She thought it again a couple of hours later when she and the doctor were having their after-supper coffee round the sitting room fire. She would miss it all when she went back to England, but she wasn't going to spoil the happy present worrying about an unknown future. As they said goodnight outside Mrs Dowling's front door the doctor said suddenly: 'We're old friends now; I find it absurd that you should call me Doctor van der Giessen— my name is Jeroen. Or do you find me too old to call me by my given name?'

'Old?' Constantia was quite taken aback. 'But you're not old—what an absurd thing to say! Of course I'll call you Jeroen.' She gave him her hand. 'I've had a lovely time, thank you.'

He held the door open for her, still holding her hand. 'I'll telephone you if I may, if it won't bore you; we could spend your next half day together.'

She nodded happily, blissfully unaware that there were to be no more half days.

# CHAPTER FOUR

SUNDAY SEEMED EMPTY; Constantia missed the children and the dogs, and most of all she missed Jeroen, but she cheered herself up with the thought that she would be seeing them all within a day or two. She bore with Mrs Dowling's ill humour, her accusations that the injections were painful, the food intolerable, Doctor Sperling neglectful; she was really quite happy. Besides, she was due to be paid in a very short while—she had spent very little of her weekly salary but had tucked it away out of sight. She had been tempted to spend it on several occasions, but she hadn't done so; she might need it to live on when she got back to England, for she could possibly have to wait a little while for the next job.

She spent the day, when she had the chance to be by herself, trying to decide what she would do when she got back to England. If she were careful she would have enough

money to take a few days' holiday, but on the
other hand she might miss a good case. A holiday could wait, she considered; after all, she
had no one to think of but herself. She sighed
at the thought and for once was glad to have
her musings interrupted by her patient, who
demanded a game of backgammon because she
was bored.

Monday began badly, with Mrs Dowling
making a fuss about her injection, declaring
that she couldn't possibly eat the breakfast she
was offered, and bemoaning a headache.

Constantia sighed silently. Mrs Dowling,
having already had her insulin, would come to
grief unless she ate her breakfast. She pointed
this out with her usual patience, to be told that
she was a fool anyway, a remark which she
ignored, merely suggesting that it might be a
good idea if Mrs Dowling took a brisk walk
to get rid of the headache—a forlorn hope, for
her patient went out of doors on only the rarest
of occasions. And as the morning wore on, the
lady's mood didn't improve. Doctor Sperling
when he came was given the sharp edge of her
tongue and got himself away as quickly as he

could, agreeing—very basely, Constantia considered—that unless his patient wished to go
out, there was no need for her to do so. Which
meant that by the afternoon, when she should
have had an hour or so to herself, Mrs Dowling
roundly averred that she could not be left on
any account.

'And you get time enough as it is,' she declared angrily, 'always out with that Doctor
van der Giessen—I wonder what you get up
to.'

Constantia didn't trust herself to answer.
She went down to the kitchen and fetched her
patient's tea. She was expected to have hers at
the same time with Mrs Dowling, but she had
no intention of doing that. She arranged the tea
tray just so and made for the door. 'Where are
you going?' demanded Mrs Dowling.

'While you have your tea I will be in my
room,' said Constantia coolly. 'I'm entitled to
some free time each day, and I haven't had it
yet.'

Safe in her room she sat down to think. Mrs
Dowling was quite impossible; tomorrow she
would see Doctor Sperling and tell him that he

would have to get another nurse. She would hate leaving Delft—she didn't allow herself to dwell on that, but she had had quite enough of her patient, who really wanted some poor meek doormat upon which to wipe her ill humour, not a trained nurse whose patience had now worn itself threadbare.

Presently she went downstairs again, removed the tray and went back to write up the diabetic chart. She had just finished it when Mrs Dowling snapped: 'I want something I can enjoy for my supper—send Nel out for a lobster. I fancy that—with a cream sauce.'

'The shops will be shutting,' Constantia pointed out, 'and although I daresay we could substitute the lobster, the cream sauce is out…too many calories.'

Mrs Dowling eyed her with dislike. 'I'll have profiteroles afterwards,' she stated, 'smothered in chocolate sauce and cream.'

Constantia put her pretty head on one side and surveyed her companion. 'You didn't much enjoy all the fuss the other day when you ate those chocolates; I'm afraid you might feel quite uncomfortable if you indulged yourself.'

Mrs Dowling threw a book at her. 'You stupid girl, always preaching at me! I'll do what I like—I always have done and I don't see why I shouldn't continue to do so. You can pack your bags and go, Nurse. You have never understood my case and you never will—I need sympathetic treatment, someone to cosset me...'

'You need a slave,' said Constantia, 'and yes, I'll go, but first I must ask you to telephone Doctor Sperling and tell him that you've dismissed me.'

'I'll let him know later—it's of no importance.'

'It is.' Constantia was being very polite. 'If you would telephone now? Or I will—I wouldn't wish to be blamed for anything that might go wrong.'

'Pooh,' observed her erstwhile patient. 'You can't frighten me. Telephone him and get out.'

Doctor Sperling sounded resigned. 'I'm sure it was through no fault of your own, Nurse,' he told her a shade pompously. 'I shall of course have to replace you.'

'Why?' asked Constantia. 'There are thousands of diabetics walking round managing very well with no nurse for miles.'

'Mrs Dowling is a private patient,' he pointed out, 'and suffers a good deal from nerves.'

'I know just how she feels,' agreed Constantia.

She packed in a few minutes; when you moved from case to case with perhaps only a day between, you learned to travel with necessities and nothing else. Mrs Dowling was lying back on her chaise-longue when she went downstairs; she had her handbag open and was fumbling around inside.

'Here's your money,' she said, and flung the notes on to the floor.

Constantia was a prudent girl; she had had to be, fending for herself, but now prudence had no chance against the splendid rage that bubbled up inside her. Nothing would have made her pick up the notes and put them in her purse. She said: 'Goodbye, Mrs Dowling,' in an icy little voice and went out of the house.

Her case was heavy and the nearest taxi rank was at the other end of the Markt. She crossed the bridge and started along Langendijk. She had forgotten that there was some sort of fair on; the streets were choked with people coming and going from the fairground and she made slow progress, hampered with her luggage—besides, she was deep in thought. She would have liked to have seen Jeroen van der Giessen before she went away, but it would be his surgery hour, and besides, what would she say to him? She would have to write him a letter...

She walked slowly on, oblivious of her surroundings, and thinking about it later she couldn't be quite sure when it was that she realised that she no longer had her handbag. Its straps still dangled neatly from her shoulder, but the bag itself was gone, and a quick search around her yielded nothing. She stood against a shop window, swallowing panic. All her money, her passport, her cheque book, had gone...

She didn't know where the police station was and when she asked a passer-by he only smiled and shook his head. She tried again, a woman this time, but she used the word station instead of bureau and the woman broke into a long explanation about trains; she paused after a minute, realising that Constantia didn't understand a word, smiled, shrugged her shoulders and walked on with a cheerful admonition in her own language.

Constantia picked up her case. She would go into a shop and ask; surely someone would understand, it was just her bad luck that she should have picked on two people who didn't…

Her case was taken quite gently out of her hand and Jeroen van der Giessen said matter-of-factly: 'You shouldn't be carrying that heavy case. And why are you carrying it?'

Constantia gulped and drew the breath that she had lost, but she didn't speak; she wasn't going to cry, and she would if she said a word just then. She stared up at him, her grey eyes wide, holding back tears.

After a few moments he said: 'Don't cry, my dear.' He had seen the cut straps still dangling from her shoulder. 'Have you any idea who or when?'

She found her voice, high and a little squeaky. 'No, I discovered it about five minutes ago. I was going to the police station, but the two people I asked to show me the way didn't understand me.'

He tucked an arm into hers and she felt much better. 'We'll go there now and you can tell me what's happened as we go. I gather Mrs Dowling no longer requires your services?'

Constantia was rapidly recovering her calm. 'She sacked me after tea; she said she wanted someone who understood her and cosseted her.' She managed a chuckle which ended in a small sniff. 'I don't think I'm much good as a private nurse.' The hard-won calm cracked a little. 'All my money was in my handbag, and my passport and...'

He was walking her rapidly through the crowded streets. 'All of which can be re-placed,' he pointed out placidly. 'Where were you going?'

'Well, back to England—where else?'

He didn't answer her but turned down a narrow side-street. 'Here we are. You don't by any chance know the number of your passport?'

She looked at him guiltily. 'It was written down in my pocketbook—it was in my bag.'

His smile was amused and very kind. 'Never mind. In you go and leave the talking to me.'

The police were kind to her and as helpful as it was possible to be. They told her, via the doctor who did the translating, that there was little hope of getting her money back, but that her passport might just possibly be thrown away. In the meantime they would notify the British Consul at The Hague.

'How much money was there?' asked the doctor.

Constantia did rapid sums in her head. 'Just over five hundred gulden, most of it in my notecase. Actually there's another week's money, but Mrs Dowling threw it at me, so I left it on the floor.' She swallowed. 'I'll have to go back for it now.'

'Oh, no, you won't,' observed the doctor strongly. 'Have you any other money at all?'

'Yes, I've some money in my bank in England.' She glanced up at him and saw that she hadn't said enough. 'About one hundred and seventy pounds.'

A muscle twitched at the corner of the doctor's mouth, but he said nothing and she went on defensively: 'It ought to be a lot more than that, but I—I used it for something important.' He didn't answer that either. 'If you would be so kind as to lend me the fare back to England...' and then stopped, appalled at the thought that perhaps he hadn't got loose money lying around and now he would have to refuse or make things difficult for himself. She went on breathlessly: 'No, I'll go back to Mrs Dowling. It's two hundred and fifty gulden—that's a lot of money—I must have been mad.'

'I said ''No'' just now,' remarked the doctor placidly, 'and I meant that. I have a much better idea. You shall come back with me; I've been wishing for someone to look after the children for quite some time.'

Constantia looked round her. They were in a small room at the police station and the two

police constables and the inspector there were
all watching them. She turned back to the doctor and said severely, 'You've just thought of
that, and it's very kind...'

He smiled very faintly. 'No, I've not just
thought of it—on the contrary, I've been thinking of nothing else for some days. And I'm not
being kind—a motherly soul to keep an eye on
those three children has become a necessity.'
He contrived to look hard-done-by as he added
in a wheedling tone, 'Just for a few weeks—
it would be very convenient for us all, and if
your passport is found it can be returned to you
at once—and the money, for that matter.' He
paused. 'And if you still want to go straight
back to England then I won't stand in your
way.'

Constantia listened to this speech with surprise, relief and a strong feeling of annoyance
at being considered motherly. Indeed, it ran-
kled her so much that she felt forced to point
out to him, with some asperity, that she had
never thought of herself as being motherly and
she doubted if she would, whereupon he observed in what she thought to be a very unfair

manner: 'Well, of course, three children are a handful—I couldn't blame you for refusing.'

'I am perfectly capable of managing three children,' she pointed out with something of a snap. 'I merely wished to make it clear that—that I'm not...'

'Motherly? I know. In that case I'll rephrase my offer. What about a small creature with brown hair and grey eyes and, I suspect, the stamina of a team of horses, joining my household?'

Perhaps being likened to a horse wasn't as bad as being described as motherly, and he had called her small. 'You're very kind,' said Constantia, 'and it would be a great help to me.'

'And to me—us. Just a minute while I talk to these men.'

They talked for some minutes and she had no idea what about, but she really didn't mind very much; she felt safe again. For the moment she had nothing to worry about; when her passport was found, if it ever would be, she would decide about going home again to England. After all, she might not fit into the doctor's life at all; the children might not like her.

A little surge of excitement turned Constantia's cheeks pink. It would be very nice to be one of a family, even if only for a little while. The doctor finished what he had to say, and she met his look with such a cheerful smile that he said: 'Good, you've recovered. Shall we go? The police will let you know the moment they hear anything, but they don't hold out much hope.'

And Constantia, rather to her surprise, discovered that she didn't really mind if they were hopeful or not.

The children were nowhere to be seen when the doctor ushered her into his house, although she could hear their voices, very faint, and the dogs barking.

'In the nursery upstairs,' explained the doctor, 'having a free-for-all before bed. Shall we go up?'

He put her case down and took her coat, tossing it with his on to a chair. A bad habit, Constantia considered; she would see that he hung his coat—and hers—up in a closet in future. Her eyes went round the noble proportions of the hall. There would be a cupboard somewhere—there were any number of doors, but she had no time to look, for he was urging her up the staircase. She stopped halfway to ask, 'Haven't you got an evening surgery?'

'Not on Mondays—I've some visits to make, though. I'll tell the children and Elisabeth can show you your room. If you could cope with their supper and bedtime, I'd be grateful.'

The children were flatteringly glad to see her and if Constantia had any doubts as to their acceptance of her, she need not have had them; they were transparently glad, and the doctor having bidden them a hasty '*Tot ziens*,' the entire party bore her down to the floor below to show her her room, shouting goodnights to their uncle as he went. Not that he went at once; first of all he took himself off to the kitchen where he spent quite a few minutes, and emerged at the end of that time looking pleased with himself, to pick up his coat and leave the house, his bag in his hand.

Constantia was struck dumb by the splendour of her room. It was not so very large, but exquisitely furnished with a golden mahogany bed covered with a rose silk spread, with the same soft colour draping the high narrow window. The carpet was silver grey and the little upholstered chair, placed so invitingly by the marble fireplace, was of grey velvet. The dressing table was mahogany too, with a triple mirror upon it, and the bedside cabinets held two charming porcelain figures holding aloft pink-shaded lamps.

She stared round her, her pretty mouth a little open. 'Is this really for me?' she asked Paul. 'There's not some mistake? I mean, it's ready for a guest—the bed's made up...'

'Oom Jeroen told us this was the room. It's a visitor's room—there are several, but this one is the prettiest.'

Elisabeth tugged at her hand. 'Here is the bathroom,' she said importantly, and opened a door by the bed, disclosing a beautifully appointed pink-tiled apartment, 'and here is a cupboard for your clotheses.'

'Clothes,' corrected Constantia. 'What super English you all speak, to be sure—you'll have to teach me to speak Dutch. Now I'll get my case and then see about your suppers, shall I?'

She beamed round at the three small faces. 'I am so pleased to be with you.'

'Us also,' declared Paul, 'most pleased.'

They all surged out of the room again, the dogs crowding close on their heels, and found Constantia's case outside the door. She supposed that the doctor had brought it upstairs before he left the house and would have picked it up and carried it back into the room, but Paul said at once: 'Girls do not carry things. I will do it, Miss…' He paused to look at her. 'What are we to call you, please?'

'Constantia, my dears, and thank you, Paul. Shall we go to the kitchen now?'

The kitchen was so clean and tidy that it seemed as though someone must have just left it exactly so. Elisabeth, holding Constantia's hand, looked round the vast place and declared: 'Rietje is not here,' and was instantly told to be quiet by her brothers.

'You have forgotten,' Pieter told her severely, 'that Rietje has gone home for the day, but you are only a little girl and cannot be expected to say things right.'

Elisabeth looked tearful. 'Rietje...' she began mulishly, so that Constantia said hastily: 'Are you going to show me what you have for your suppers? It would be such a help to me if you would, Elisabeth.'

The little girl bustled importantly over to the Aga and the two boys, without being asked, began to lay the table. There was soup on the stove that smelt delicious, so that Constantia wrinkled her nose, savouring it. She dished it up, sat the children round the table, cut the bread and butter and sat with them while they ate. They had good manners, answering her questions readily and helping her to clear the table when they had finished.

'What about the dogs?' she asked, stacking the plates at the enormous double sink.

'We feed them now,' explained Paul, 'and Elisabeth feeds Butch the cat.'

So Constantia washed up while the children saw to the animals, and presently they all went upstairs again to the nursery. There was still a few minutes before bedtime; Constantia, happier than she had been for a very long time, sat down on the floor with the three of them around her and the dogs worming their way in where they could, and rendered a shortened version of Robin Hood before whisking Elisabeth off to bath and bed with a firm admonishment to the boys to do the same.

She had just succeeded in getting them all safely tucked up for the night when the doctor returned. He had come in very quietly and Constantia hadn't heard him mount the stairs. She was being half strangled by Elisabeth's embrace when he said from the door:

'Decidedly motherly, I should have said. I see that you have coped excellently.' He strolled into the room and sat down on his niece's bed. 'I expect you would like to go and unpack and so forth while I say goodnight to the children. Shall we meet in the sitting room in about ten minutes' time?'

Ten minutes to repair the ravages of three small children would be welcome. Constantia went off to her beautiful room and sat down before the dressing table, not attempting to unpack. She had the feeling that if she were still wanted, she would stay in this lovely house for as long as she well could. Presently, after a very perfunctory tidying of herself, she went downstairs.

The doctor wasn't in the sitting room, so she sat down to wait for him, happily unaware that both boys were out of their beds and in their sister's room, squashed up on her bed with their uncle, while the dogs jostled for the best place on the rug.

'Listen carefully, my dears,' Doctor van der Giessen was saying. 'We are going to continue with our little conspiracy…'

Constantia was curled up in one of the big chairs by the open hearth when he came into the sitting room. He looked unhurried, placid, and wore the friendly air of an old family friend or a member of the family—if she had had one. Perhaps that was why she liked him so much, she thought fleetingly as he settled himself in the great winged chair opposite her own.

He sat for a few moments saying nothing at all, and she sat quiet too. He would be tired after his day; probably he wanted to mull over his cases. The doctor was mulling, but not about any of his patients, but presently he said:

'What a fortunate thing that I should have met you this evening. You cannot imagine how relieved I am.'

She said rather shyly: 'Well, I expect you've found three children rather a handful—I can't think how you managed.'

His voice was bland. 'Which is just as well.' He got up and went over to a console table against one wall. 'What will you have to drink? Sherry?'

She knew nothing at all about wines; her aunt had offered an indifferent sherry to her rare guests and Constantia, treated to a glass, hadn't thought much of it. In hospital, of course, if one went out for the evening with one of the young doctors, one was mostly given a lager and not asked. Once or twice she had spent an evening out with a registrar, and not knowing that not all sherries were like her aunt's, had asked for Dubonnet; she hadn't liked that very much either. The doctor watched her hesitating and said blandly: 'Try a medium sherry. If you don't like it you can have something else.'

It was like golden velvet on her tongue, and she took an appreciative sip and said, 'Oh, this is lovely—I didn't know sherry could taste different.'

He had poured himself a Genever and sat down again. He didn't smile but said: 'Er—yes, they do vary enormously.'

She eyed the well-stocked silver tray with an unconsciously questioning gaze, and he went on smoothly: 'The owner of this house kindly allows me the run of his cellars.'

She took another sip. 'He must be a poppet—I should like to meet him,' and then, afraid that she had vexed him, 'I'm sorry, I shouldn't have said that—it's none of my business.'

'You shall meet him one day, Constantia. How pleasant it is to have someone to talk to.'

'Oh, would you like to talk? Have you had a busy day? Do you have a great many patients?'

'Yes, I've been busy and I do have quite a number of patients—quite a few of them live in the surrounding villages. The older ones don't go to the doctor as often as they should, and quite often when they call me I can't do very much for them.'

'There was one today?' she asked quickly.

'Yes, an old man…'

The doctor talked well and Constantia was a good listener, moreover she asked the right questions and understood what he was saying; it was some considerable time later that he looked at the carved Friesian clock on the wall and observed: 'I've been boring on and on, and you must be famished. Let's get some supper.'

She got to her feet at once. 'Look, stay here, I'm sure I can manage in the kitchen. There was some soup left over from the children's meal, and there are bound to be eggs and cheese…'

'Rietje will have left something—soup, yes, and a *quiche lorraine* in the *ijs kast*—there'll be a salad, too, and some kind of pudding.'

She was at the door. 'I'll call you when it's ready,' she said, happy to be useful.

The soup was simmering nicely, and the *quiche*, which she considered looked quite *cordon bleu*, was quickly in the oven. The salad was already mixed in a beautiful china bowl and there was a caramel custard too. Constantia, whistling cheerfully to herself, laid the table, put the plates to warm, peered at the *quiche* and went in search of the doctor.

He was still sitting where she had left him, his eyes shut. He opened them as she went in, however, and she said contritely: 'I'm sorry, you were asleep.'

He shook his head. 'No—dreaming.' He got to his feet and stretched hugely. 'There's a bottle of Moselle, did you find it?'

'No, but then I didn't look for it.' She hesitated. 'Isn't that a white wine? Shouldn't it be chilled?'

He was strolling beside her across the hall. 'Quite right. I'll wring Rietje's neck if she's forgotten to put it in the *ijs kast*.'

It was there all right. They had their soup and then, while Constantia dished the *quiche*, he opened the wine and poured it into two beautifully engraved glasses.

'This is a very nice wine,' said Constantia, 'it's rather like the parsnip wine my aunt used to make.'

The doctor suppressed a shudder at her description of his really splendid Lieserer Niederberg Sussenberg, and observed mildly that he had never had the pleasure of sampling parsnip wine.

'Well, it's easy to make and it doesn't cost much,' said Constantia helpfully, nicely relaxed, what with having a roof over her head and a well-cooked meal inside her, not to mention the sherry and the Moselle. 'If you like, I could make some for you.'

A spasm passed over her companion's handsome features. 'That would be delightful, but would you have the time?' he wanted to know. 'And that reminds me, we have a good deal to discuss. Routine first, I think.'

He became businesslike and very precise, making her quickly conversant with the running of his house, the comings and goings of the children and his own irregular hours. 'I do try and have breakfast with them, but it doesn't always work out that way. You'll find Rietje in the kitchen about seven o'clock, though, and if I'm not here she's to see them off to school—now you'll be able to do that, if you will.'

As far as she could make out, her days were going to be well-filled, if not downright busy, for meals would have to be kept hot, children dealt with, and the housework done as well as the shopping. Just for a moment Constantia felt daunted, and it must have shown on her face, for the doctor said: 'It's not nearly as bad as it sounds. Rietje gets through a great deal of work and if you like she'll do the shopping. There's a niece who comes in to do the washing, too.' He smiled at her encouragingly. 'If you'll see to the children…?'

'Yes, of course, and anything else—it's a very large house, isn't it? I've only seen some of it, but looking after it must take up hours of time.'

'We don't use all the rooms.' He cleared the plates and fetched their pudding and poured some more wine for them both. 'Now, as regards your salary. Would the same amount as Mrs Dowling gave you be agreeable to you?'

'Salary? I don't want any money. Gracious, Doctor van der Giessen, you've taken me in and given me a home, just like that—I'm an extra mouth to feed and extra work and washing. I'm very grateful for that, and even if the police don't get my money back, I'll go round to Mrs Dowling and get my last week's salary and that will be enough to get back to England.'

'I'll see to that for you, Constantia, but I hope very much that even if your passport is returned you will stay with us for a little while. I have no idea where to start looking for someone; I'm not even sure what she would be called.'

He served her with a second helping of pudding and sat back in his chair. 'And another thing, why am I suddenly Doctor van der Giessen? I thought I had become Jeroen.'

Her grey eyes twinkled at him. 'You sounded a bit like Doctor van der Giessen.' She added vaguely: 'Salaries and things, you know.'

He laughed. 'I'm sorry. But what I said stands; you'll work very hard, you know, and I daresay you'll not get much time to yourself during the day.'

She said a little wistfully, 'I shall like that. I've often wondered what it would be like to live with a large family, and dogs and cats and children running in and out.'

'Were none of your cases with families?'

Constantia shook her head. 'No—all of them lonely and unhappy and far too rich.' She pointed out: 'It was because they had so much money that they were unhappy, I expect. I couldn't live with someone like that, you know.' She paused and added carefully: 'I'd rather not have any money, Jeroen; Mrs Dowling said…well, she said that you hadn't any, and three children to see to…'

The doctor's placid face remained placid, only his eyes gleamed very bright. 'Now, I wonder how she got to hear about that?'

'I've no idea, but if it's true—and we are friends, you said so—then it would be most unfair…'

He strolled over to the sink with their plates and she began to clear the table. 'I'll tell you what,' he said, 'I'll let you know if I'm pressed for cash and we can trim your salary accordingly.'

And with that she had to be content.

They washed up together and then went upstairs to have their coffee in the sitting room and when presently Constantia tidied the lovely little Meissen cups on to the tray with its silver coffee pot, the doctor said: 'You said you hadn't seen the whole of the house. Shall we go round it now?'

It wasn't late and she wasn't tired, so she went with him out into the hall, and when he opened a door behind the sitting room she went in. It was a small room with a long narrow window, furnished with one or two small armchairs, a drum table, a worktable and an inlaid cabinet along one wall. It had a needlework carpet on the floor and thick silk curtains of the same shade at the window; the furniture was of the Regency period, very delicate and graceful, and yet somehow the room was restful and cosy.

'Oh, what a dear little room!' declared Constantia, quite enchanted. 'I can just imagine sitting here…'

'As often as you like,' promised her host, and when she protested that she hadn't meant that at all, said: 'But I do, Constantia.'

He led the way through a double door, ornately carved, which opened on to a small balcony with steps leading down to yet another room. A large apartment, this, its walls lined with bookshelves and with comfortable red leather chairs arranged around circular tables decorated with marquetry. Constantia, who liked reading, heaved a great sigh.

'How super,' she breathed, 'all those books—though I suppose they're in Dutch.'

'Not all of them—there are quite a few English works. You'll find them in the catalogue on the centre table.'

'It's all very grand, isn't it? And yet it's a home too. Mrs Dowling has enormous rooms and a great deal of hideous furniture, and it isn't home at all.'

Jeroen merely smiled and led her down the steps to the floor of the library and through another, very small door in one of its panelled walls. They were in a narrow passage now, one arm leading back to the hall, the other to the back of the house. The doctor turned down it and opened a door at its end; a conservatory, a fairy-land of spring flowers and shrubs.

'Do you have a gardener?' asked Constantia, awed.

'Yes—the owner likes it to be maintained. We'll go along here and through the other door.' Which led into what she rightly guessed to be a ballroom, all white and gold and with an elaborately painted ceiling. She had no words for it as the doctor opened another door into the dining room, in the Palladian style and furnished in the early Georgian manner. It had an eye-catching chimneypiece of green and white marble, elaborately inlaid with coloured marbles. 'Very old,' the doctor pointed out, 'sixteenth century. I find it ugly—it's from Milan.'

They went back into the hall and he opened the last door. 'We don't use this often,' he observed, and really she wasn't surprised. The tables and chairs were delicate and gilded, with needlework seats, and the carpet was a huge Aubusson in faded pastels; the curtains were

brocade, heavily fringed and looped elaborately.

'One would wear one's very best dress
here,' remarked Constantia, 'pearls, of course,
one or two gorgeous rings, and earrings too.
Silver-grey silk organza, I think, embroidered
with little pink flowers. It would cost hundreds
of pounds.'

Again the doctor said nothing but led her
back to the hall once more. They were starting
for the staircase when the telephone rang. It
was on the wall in the passage leading away
from the hall and she could hear his voice,
decisive and firm, and she wasn't surprised
when he came back to her to say: 'I have to
go out, I'm afraid. I'll see you in the morning—we'll go over the rest of the house tomorrow.'

She nodded and said goodnight quietly, and
when he had gone she went back to the sitting
room and fetched the coffee tray. The kitchen
gleamed cosily as she went in; she washed the
cups and saucers carefully, rubbed up the coffee pot and its accompanying sugar bowl and

cream jug, and took herself off to bed. But mindful of her new duties, before she climbed into her pretty bed, she padded upstairs to make sure that the children were asleep.

# CHAPTER FIVE

THE DOCTOR WASN'T at breakfast. Constantia, down in good time, found a tall, stout woman with a cheerful face and bright blue eyes in the kitchen. She appeared to be of middle age, but her hair was so pale that it was difficult to see if it was grey or blonde. Constantia went to her at once, holding out her hand. 'You must be Rietje—I'm Constantia Morley.'

The woman smiled and shook hands and said something in her own language. Constantia couldn't understand any of it, but there was no need; the business of getting breakfast ready was well understood by them both. She cut bread, poured glasses of milk and set the table and then went upstairs to see if the children were ready. The boys were, but Elisabeth was still putting on her shoes, her fair hair in a tangle. Constantia buttoned the shoes, reduced the tangle to shining smoothness, kissed the little face under the fringe and hurried everyone downstairs. The next half an hour was an organised rush, culminating in her walking down the pretty little garden behind the house and seeing the three children safely into the street.

She and Rietje had another cup of coffee in peace and quiet then, and Constantia managed to convey her wish to wash up and tidy the kitchen—a decision which Rietje seemed to welcome, for she had the cooking to do.

'I'll make the beds, too,' said Constantia, and then struggled with her few words of Dutch to make herself understood. It surprised and delighted her that after a few false starts, they understood each other very well; Rietje was kind and patient and good-humoured, and they laughed together over Constantia's mistakes before they separated; Rietje to the store cupboard and Constantia to the sink.

She had just finished the last of the dishes when the doctor came in. He was in slacks and a sweater and badly in need of a shave, but his eyes were as blue and clear as they always were and his face wore its usual calm expression.

'Coffee?' asked Constantia instantly, 'and breakfast in a brace of shakes…'

'My dear girl, I have surgery to take in twenty minutes—I must have a bath and shave.'

'You'll faint in your bath if you don't eat,' Constantia assured him firmly. 'Here's your coffee, so sit down and drink it. I'll make some toast and boil you an egg.' She remembered the size of him. 'Two eggs.'

He did as she had bidden him and as she refilled his cup she asked: 'A baby? It usually is at night.'

He buttered the toast she had handed him and spread it lavishly with marmalade. 'A little boy with a good old-fashioned croup—laringeal stridor to you. Very nasty, but he's out of the wood now, I think.'

'Hospital?'

He nodded. 'Yes. His parents have a farm—rather isolated, so hospital seemed the best thing.' He began on his second slice. 'How very pleasant it is to come home to someone who asks me what I've been doing and understands when I tell her.'

Constantia pinkened. She said lamely: 'Well, you know how it is when you're a nurse...'

'I don't, actually,' he was laughing at her mildly, 'but I can guess—anyway, it's nice for me.' He pushed back his chair. 'Thanks for the breakfast. Did the children get to school?'

'On time,' she told him. 'What a marvellous person Rietje is. We even understand each other, or rather she understands my dozen or so words.' She added kindly: 'Now run along and change. There'll be coffee for you after surgery; Rietje wrote it all down. Do go.'

He grinned at her from the doorway. 'A little dragon,' he told her, 'that's what you are. There's one in my study; you're its twin.'

Constantia made the beds and tidied the bedrooms, and accompanied by Rietje, peeped into the other rooms which opened on to the gallery on the first floor. They were very splendid, she considered, each with its own colour scheme, the furniture polished as though each had an occupant; Rietje must work like a slave. She mentioned it to the doctor after his morning surgery and she went upstairs with the coffee tray to his study. 'If you paid me half the money you want me to have, you could afford to have a daily woman in—Rietje must be worn to death.'

He poured his coffee and asked: 'Where is your cup?'

'I'll have mine downstairs later.'

'You'll have it now, with me.' He went to a Friesian wall cupboard, opened its glass-fronted doors, took out a delicate Meissen cup and saucer and handed it to her.

'Oh, no—I can't,' declared Constantia. 'I shall drop it or something awful.'

For answer he poured the coffee and handed her the cup and saucer and said: 'Sit down, do.' And when she had done so: 'I'll do my visits next. I'll be lunching out; I've someone to see in den Haag, but I'll be back for the evening surgery and my visits. With luck I'll be home about seven o'clock—perhaps eight.'

'No tea?' she asked.

'Someone will give me a cup, I daresay. I'd like coffee after surgery, though, if you could manage that; I try and squeeze half an hour out for the children before they go to bed. Will you be all right?'

She nodded. 'Where's the dragon?'

He got up without speaking and went back to the Friesian wall cupboard again, then crossed the room to put into her hand a small fierce-looking dragon, most exquisitely modelled in porcelain with a sepia pattern.

'The earliest Delft china,' he explained. 'Exquisite, isn't it? Not fierce at all if you look closely at it; it's almost smiling.'

She cradled the beautiful thing in her hands. 'It's out of this world,' she exclaimed. 'Of course it belongs to the owner of this house?'

'Indeed it does.' His voice was bland. 'He sets great store by his family possessions.'

She stroked the dragon's head. 'And quite right too. But how do you know it's a she?'

His voice was still bland. 'I didn't—not until a little while ago in the kitchen. I noticed a distinct resemblance.'

She laughed and handed it back to him. 'That's absurd, but thank you for letting me hold her. Is there anything I can do to help you?'

'Don't tell me there's time on those small hands of yours. No, nothing at the moment. I have a very capable secretary who comes in each morning.' He smiled suddenly. 'But if she's unable to come for any reason, then you may find yourself filling yet another gap.'

Constantia finished her coffee and got up. 'Rietje is going to show me where everything is in the kitchen—just in case she isn't here some time or other. I expect I'll see you later.'

He opened the door for her and she went through it with the tray carefully balanced, her mind already busy with the small chores to be done before the children got home for their dinners.

It was that afternoon, when she came back early from walking the dogs and found the house quiet, that she wandered into the sitting room. Rietje had disappeared, gone home, Constantia presumed, the three dogs had settled down in their baskets for their afternoon snooze, and Constantia felt a little lonely. She circled the room, looking at the portraits on the walls—ancestors, she presumed; ladies with

corkscrew curls and rich silk dresses, gentlemen staring at her from the canvas, their blue
eyes and high-bridged noses reminding her
forcibly of the doctor. Uncles and aunts, she
thought vaguely, and remembered that there
was a tear in Elisabeth's anorak.

She could mend it, and possibly tidy the
children's clothes as well. She went into the
hall and made for the staircase and came face
to face with a short spare man of middle age,
bearing a tray loaded with what she recognised
as the massive silver set out on the side table
in the dining room. A thief? The owner of the
house desirous of retrieving his more precious
possessions? She came to a halt and asked in
her halting Dutch, *'Wie bent U?'* and added,
*'Goeden middag,'* just in case he wasn't a
thief.

It was a little disconcerning to be answered
in almost perfect English. 'Good afternoon,
miss. I am sorry if I have startled you.' He
paused and went on: 'The owner likes me to
polish the silver each week. The doctor may
have forgotten to tell you.'

She smiled her relief. 'Oh, he did, but then he was up most of the night and busy this morning. Can I do anything to help, and would you like a cup of tea?'

'Thank you, no, miss. Rietje will have left the coffee ready on the stove should I require a cup. My name is Tarnus.'

She smiled again. 'Well, Mr Tarnus, don't let me hinder you.' She started for the stairs again and then turned round to ask: 'Does the owner of this house ever come here? It's such a beautiful place, I don't know how he can bear to be away from it. If—when you see him, please will you tell him how absolutely super it is?'

Mr Tarnus's rather solemn face cracked into a smile. 'Indeed I will, miss.'

'He won't know who I am—Doctor van der Giessen asked me to be mother's help while the children are staying here. I—I had just left another job.'

Her companion bowed his head slightly. 'I'm sure the children will be delighted to have you here, miss. There is a great deal to do in the house now that they are here.'

'Yes, I'm sure there is. Rietje is showing me how best to help, and they're such very good children and most careful of everything in the house.'

'So I understand, miss.'

She started up the staircase. 'Well, goodbye, Mr Tarnus.'

'Goodbye, miss.' He went on his way and she, watching him, thought that he looked like a rather super butler, the kind one saw on the films, and which she had never quite believed were true to life.

The children came tumbling in at teatime, laughing and shouting and wanting their tea and then her help with their simple homework. Elisabeth had no homework, of course, so she sat quietly, dressing her dolls while Constantia and the boys sat at the nursery table, doing arithmetic. And when they had finished, Constantia found a jigsaw puzzle to keep them busy while she examined the dolls' wardrobes and promised a new dress or two for the dolls.

'I'll go and buy some stuff tomorrow,' she promised. 'Pink, I think, don't you? And perhaps a knitted cap and scarf—it's still chilly…' She gave Elisabeth a hug because she was a nice cuddly little girl and the pair of them went to help with the puzzle. They were all crouched on the floor, working away at it, when the doctor came in.

The room at once became a happy chaos of children and dogs with the doctor in the centre; he bore his small relatives' greetings with placid good humour, made much of the dogs and then turned to Constantia.

He was tired, she saw that immediately, although he was immaculately turned out; she found herself wondering who cleaned his shoes and pressed his suits. Rietje perhaps, although how could she find the time?

He was speaking to her and she wasn't listening. 'I'm terribly sorry,' she said, 'I was thinking about something…'

'Nothing important,' his tone was casual, 'I only wanted to know how you had found your first day as—what was it? Mother's help.'

'I've enjoyed every minute of it. You're tired, would you like some coffee?'

He shook his head. 'I've some work to do— I'll be in the study if you want me, but I'll stay here for a little while. I expect you'd like to get the children's supper.'

She agreed cheerfully, although she would have liked to have stayed, but after all, she wasn't a member of the family; they had admitted her to their circle with ready friendliness, but that didn't mean that she could abuse it. She went to the kitchen and got the simple meal ready—milk and biscuits, for the children had had a big tea. She set the dinner Rietje had made ready in the oven, too, and went along to the dining room to set the table.

Rietje had advised her to do that; the kitchen, in her opinion, was no place in which the doctor should eat his dinner. Constantia wasn't quite sure if she was supposed to share it with him—true, she had done so previously, but that might have been kindness on his part so that she would feel at home. She would have to find out, and what better time to do so than the present?

She went back to the nursery and found that he had taken her place on the floor, doing the jigsaw with the children. He looked up as she went in and enquired: 'Supper ready?' He got to his feet and went on, 'I'm off to my study.'

Constantia stood in the doorway. 'I'm not sure about something,' she said in a little rush. 'Rietje said I was to give you dinner in the dining room, that you mustn't eat in the kitchen—at least, I'm sure that's what she said. Do—do you like to have it alone? I mean, I know I had dinner with you last night, but then it was the first day and I expect you wanted me to feel at home. But if you usually eat your dinner alone I daresay you'd prefer it.'

He heard her out without interruption. 'Constantia, I should have made myself clear before this. Of course we will take our meals together—regard it as part of your job if you wish, for I shall undoubtedly pour out the day's troubles into your ears. Moreover, I shall expect intelligent comments. As for Rietje, she's a tyrant.'

'Oh, she's not,' declared Constantia warmly, 'she's wonderful and quite right—of course you must take your meals in the dining room now I'm here to help. She couldn't possibly have managed on her own, but I'm another pair of hands and now there's no reason why you shouldn't.'

He dropped a gentle hand on to her shoulder. 'Very fierce,' he observed. 'If the little Delft dragon would smile—'

Constantia smiled, feeling suddenly absurdly light-hearted.

'That's better. Are we dining at the usual time?'

'Yes. Shall I let you know? You'll be in your study?'

'Please. I'll say goodnight to this lot and leave you to cope.'

It was exactly half-past seven when she tapped on the study door. The children had been good, but like all children, very lively, especially at bedtime. She had just had the time to go to her room and tidy herself and change from the tweed skirt and sweater she had worn all day to one of the two dresses she had with her; a brown corduroy pinafore dress with a fine pink woollen blouse under it. She found the doctor sitting back in his chair, his large feet on the desk, an untidy mess of papers scattered around him. The desk was an enormous one, beautiful Chinese lacquer with a tooled leather top and a great number of drawers on either side, and looking at it, Constantia had the strong feeling that despite the scattering of papers, if she were to look inside those drawers they would be in apple-pie order. There were, she thought, two sides to the doctor—his worn-out car and well-worn sheepskin jacket were in direct contradiction to his expensive tailored clothes and the well-polished shoes; his casual, cheerful manner hid, she fancied, a very determined and resourceful mind.

He got to his feet, scattering even more papers, as she went in and she found herself going a little pink at his: 'You look nice—I like that thing. You have no idea how pleasant it is to have a mother's help about the place.'

'How did you manage?' she wanted to know.

'Oh, I caught up on my reading and notes and so on, at night.' Jeroen spoke casually. 'We'll have a drink, shall we?'

She had done her best with dinner. The dining room looked welcoming, with the pink-shaded wall sconces casting a glow over the table laid with the silver and fragile china and glass. She had brought up the food from the kitchen as Rietje had suggested, and put it on the hot plate hidden behind a screen in a corner of the room; lobster soup, steak grilled with black peppers, baby new potatoes and broccoli. Rietje was a magnificent cook. There was a fresh fruit salad for dessert and the coffee tray was ready in the kitchen. Constantia saw with pleasure that the doctor was pleased. He went away and came back presently with a bottle of claret, remarking that only the best wine in the cellar was worthy of such an occasion.

'I didn't cook it,' she told him, 'Rietje did all that, I just laid the table. Oh, that reminds me; I met a man in the hall this afternoon, he had all the silver on a tray. He spoke English and I liked him, he said he was called Tarnus and came to clean the silver for the owner.' She was helping herself to potatoes and didn't look up to see the expression on her companion's face. 'I expect you know him.'

'Er—yes,' agreed Jeroen. 'He's been with the family for some considerable time. He considers the silvercleaning one of his most important tasks.'

'I expect he likes doing it—it's so lovely. Perhaps he hasn't enough to do for your...the owner?'

The doctor said smoothly, 'Very probably.' And after a pause: 'I usually take the dogs for a walk after dinner.'

Perhaps she was asking too many questions, Constantia thought uneasily, or did he find her boring company after all? She said rather too hastily: 'Do you want your coffee first or when you come in?'

'Before I go, please. Would you like to come with us?'

Now he was being polite. She said stiffly: 'No, thank you, it's been quite a long day, but I've enjoyed it...'

She made polite conversation while they drank their coffee in the sitting room, and when he had gone with the dogs, whisked herself back to the dining room to clear away their meal. She had washed up, terrified of breaking something, and was setting the table for the children's breakfast in the kitchen when he returned. His 'What are you doing?' seemed to her to be a little unnecessary, but she answered him equably.

'Getting ready for the morning.'

His eyes swept round the room. 'Where are the dinner things?'

'Washed up and put away. I was very careful; Rietje showed me where everything goes.'

'I didn't intend you to wash the dishes, Constantia. They would have been cleared in the morning.'

She looked at him in surprise. 'Well, I could wait until the morning if you wish, but it's much easier to wash up directly a meal's over, you know. Besides, there are the breakfast things to do in the morning and the children to see to. But of course I'll leave them if you want me to.' She bent to pat Prince's head.

'You make me sound like a tyrant,' said the doctor. 'In future we'll do the dishes together and share the dogs' walk, unless you're too tired.'

She looked across the room and smiled at him. 'That would be nice—and I'm never tired. But don't you have things to do in the evenings? I mean, go out with friends or something?' She stopped herself. 'How silly of me; of course you couldn't get out because of the children. Well, you can now, for I'll be here.'

He smiled but didn't say anything and she thought, rather crossly, that she knew almost nothing about him; his family, his friends, his work. That he was a contented man seemed obvious, but surely he wouldn't be quite happy to live in someone else's house for the rest of his life, maybe—? And he wasn't married; perhaps there was a girl, though. Constantia pictured someone tall and stately and beautiful, sweeping round the lovely old house in beautiful clothes, although if the doctor was as poor as Mrs Dowling had said, she might have to make those for herself.

The silence was lasting too long; so she said briskly: 'I think I'll say goodnight—I expect you've some work to do.'

'I did it before dinner,' he responded. 'I was hoping for half an hour of your company, but if you're tired...?' He left the question in the air for her to answer.

'Shall I make some more coffee?' she asked happily.

'That would be nice. I'll come with you and carry the tray.'

So they spent an hour together, and Constantia, led on by her companion's casual questions, told him about her aunt and the rather unpleasant woman who had taken possession of her home. 'I couldn't stay,' she explained. 'I felt as though I was trespassing.'

'An unpleasant person. You were comfortable at the hospital?'

Looking back on it, she agreed that she had been comfortable. Her room had been adequate, she had had a number of friends and never lacked for invitations in her off-duty, and she had done quite well in her work, but it was only now that she realised that she hadn't been happy. Something had been missing, that was why she had left the hospital and joined an agency. She forbore from saying so, though. She had, she decided, been talking too much. She got up and collected the coffee cups and made a polite little speech about being grateful and hoping that she hadn't taken up his time, and assured him that she would be delighted to mind the children in the evenings if he wished to return to his normal social life.

She was surprised at his shout of laughter. 'I do believe you're trying to marry me off, Constantia—I can't think of any other reason for your enthusiasm for sending me out in the evenings. But joking apart, I shall be glad of a chance to renew one or two of my evening outings.'

He came and took the tray from her and bore it to the kitchen and stayed to help her clear it away. In the hall she wished him good-night, and because he reminded her, added *Jeroen*. She was half way up the staircase when he called after her.

'Thank you, Constantia, for all you have done today. I hope it's a good augury for the future. Do you feel that you can bear to stay?'

She turned to look at him. He was leaning against the carved banisters, his hands in his pockets; he looked solid and safe and very handsome.

'Yes, I'll stay,' she told him.

*    *    *

The days followed each other with astonishing rapidity. There was no news of Constantia's passport or of her money and bag, but somehow that didn't seem to matter very much. The police had it in hand, they had said, and there was nothing to do but be patient. The children, getting to know her, became a shade naughtier but nonetheless delightful, and she was rapidly picking up a few words of Dutch. The children delighted in teaching her for one thing, and Rietje took pains to tell her the names of everything she came across in the kitchen and during her chores around the house. The doctor she saw for only a short time each day; she had been a little disappointed when he had taken her at her word and spent two or three successive evenings out. She wondered where he went, for on each occasion he had changed into a dinner jacket, left her to eat her solitary dinner and returned long after she had gone up to bed. He must have a great many friends, she decided, after all, and she had in all fairness urged him to return to his usual life now that the children were in her care.

But at the end of the week, on Saturday, he stayed home. They all went for a walk in the afternoon and had a noisy tea in the kitchen afterwards, and then went upstairs to the nursery and played spillikins with the children. They went to bed a little later because there was no school in the morning and when at last Constantia had chivvied them lovingly to their beds and tucked them up for the night, she went down to the kitchen where, as usual, Rietje had left a beautifully cooked meal ready for her to warm up. The doctor had disappeared—back to the children, she discovered, hearing distant squeals of laughter coming from the top of the house.

And on Sunday he stayed home too, appearing at breakfast a little late because he had taken the dogs for their walk first, and then organising everyone to wash up and make beds so that they could all go to church. Constantia, who had suggested that she might be excused from joining them, was swept up to her room, bidden to put on her outdoors things and then borne downstairs again without quite knowing how it had happened, although she was glad it had.

They sat in a row in a high-backed pew, and the children were almost too well-behaved to be true; their shrill treble voices deafened her on one side, while the doctor's deep boom obliterated all sound from the other. She sat through the unintelligible sermon contentedly enough, Elisabeth's small hand tucked into hers, while her thoughts wandered happily over the past week. It had been one of the best weeks of her life, she concluded, and sensing Jeroen's eyes upon her, turned to smile at him.

It was at breakfast on Monday that he announced that he would be away for the whole of that day and return the following morning. His instructions to Constantia were clear and concise, and over and above them he told her that Tarnus would be sleeping in the house, Rietje too.

'Oh, but I'm not in the least nervous,' she assured him, 'there's really no need.'

'But *I* am nervous, and there is a need,' he observed placidly. 'Can you cope with the dogs as well, do you think?'

She assured him that she could and would, and added after a moment's hesitation: 'I hope you have a nice time.'

He smiled. 'I'm sure I shall. There's a telephone number on my desk—if you need me urgently you can reach me, or someone will take a message.'

He nodded casually, embraced the children, bade the dogs goodbye and went out of the house, which suddenly seemed unnaturally quiet. Which, seeing that he was a very quiet man, didn't make sense.

The day seemed long and the evening, after the children had been put to bed, even longer. Constantia sat in the lovely sitting room, fashioning dolls' clothes for Elisabeth's family of dolls, and felt lonely.

'And this will never do,' she told herself, glad to hear a voice, even if it was her own. 'Remember this is a temporary job, my girl, so don't get too wrapped up in it. As soon as your passport is found you'll have no excuse to stay, and even if Jeroen wants you to, I think you'll do better in England.' The tones in which she uttered this statement sounded doubtful. 'There must be plenty of home helps in Delft,' she mused, still out loud, 'and I'm sure he expects me to leave.'

She sighed and went to the kitchen to wish Rietje and Mr Tarnus goodnight. They were sitting one each side of the Aga. Rietje was knitting, Mr Tarnus had on a pair of spectacles and was reading the paper. They looked like an old married couple. They got to their feet as she went in and chorused, '*Wel te rusten*' and when she offered to set the table for breakfast she was firmly, but kindly, refused. She could hear the murmur of their voices as she went back to the hall, into the sitting room to fetch her sewing and turn off the lamps, and then upstairs to bed.

Jeroen would be back in the morning, she reminded herself as she yawned her way to her room. The day had seemed flat without him, although heaven knew she saw very little of him, but somehow his presence was very strong in the house even when he wasn't there. 'One would think that he owned the place!' she muttered as she brushed her hair.

The doctor returned shortly after the children had left for school. Constantia, who had got up early and taken the dogs for a quick walk before breakfast because they expected it, had washed up and started on the children's beds when she heard his step on the stair.

She looked over her shoulder, a pillow between her teeth while she shook it into a clean case, and saw him in the doorway. Her hullo was necessarily muffled but nonetheless pleased. She dropped the pillow on to the bed, thumped it well and asked: 'Did you have a good time? Would you like breakfast or coffee? I forgot to ask you if you had a surgery this morning—it's almost half-past eight.'

He crossed the room, laughing, and caught her by the shoulders. 'You're being a dragon again, firing questions at me. Don't worry about surgery, someone's taking it for me. And yes, I've had breakfast and I'll have coffee later, when surgery's finished. Did you miss me?'

She stared at him blankly. 'Yes, I did,' and added quickly, 'we all did.'

'Your passport has been found. The police telephoned me—it was in a ditch by the side of the main road to den Haag. They're holding it for fingerprints and so on, but you'll have it back very shortly.'

She was conscious of bitter disappointment because now she was free to go back to England, back to her lonely life. She faltered: 'Oh, good.'

'Excellent.' Jeroen was leaning over the end of the bed, watching her while she fiddled with the sheets. 'Now you can go back to England.'

'So I can.' Her voice was very bright.

'But I'd like you to come back here, Constantia—it has occurred to me that it might be a very good idea if we were to marry.'

# CHAPTER SIX

CONSTANTIA WENT PINK and then white, her grey eyes enormous in her surprised face. 'Marry you?' she squeaked. 'But we don't—I don't, that is...'

'You don't love me?' he finished in a perfectly ordinary voice. 'But I haven't mentioned love, have I, dear girl? I believe that we like each other, and that is important, you know—we enjoy the same things and laugh at the same things too, and we have pleasure in each other's company—all these things make for a happy marriage. You have no family and no ties and as far as I can make out, a lonely future; I have a large family scattered around but who will nonetheless be delighted to welcome you. I have been nagged about marrying for some years now, and until now I haven't thought much about it.'

He paused. 'I suppose I was waiting...' He shrugged his shoulders and came to stand before her, smiling down into her startled, puzzled face. 'Love doesn't need to come into it, my dear—not yet, at any rate. You shall have all the time in the world to get used to the idea of being my wife, I'll not hurry you—we can have what one could term a friendly arrangement. If it doesn't work out between us then there's no harm done and you will be free to go. Divorce is easy these days.'

Constantia stared up at his calm face—he didn't appear in the least bit excited, and she felt chilled at his casual manner. She said in a small voice: 'If you can talk about divorce like that, you can't be serious.'

'I'm serious, Constantia,' he contradicted, 'I don't care for divorce, I said that so that you would understand that I wouldn't hold you to a marriage which had become unhappy—you might fall in love.'

'So might you.'

'I'm thirty-nine and I've been in and out of love a good many times, but that isn't quite the same thing as loving someone. But you're a child still and lovely to look at—I can't think why you haven't been snapped up...'

She smiled a little. 'I didn't want to be snapped up, as you so elegantly put it. It's true I'm a little afraid of being lonely, but that's not a good reason to marry, is it?'

Jeroen had taken one of her hands in his and was idly examining it. 'On the contrary, it's a very good one, provided there are other good reasons too. You would not mind to live in Delft; to be a doctor's wife and put up with delayed meals and broken appointments and...?'

'Oh, no. I think...' She stopped and gave him an honest look. 'I know that I should like it. I love the town and the house and this kind of life. I could be happy, and I would try and be a good companion to you and help you all I could. Would—would you go on living in this house? If we married, would the owner object to me being here too?'

There was a gleam, quickly damped down, in the blue eyes. 'I'm quite sure that he will be very happy about it.'

'And the children?'

'Oh, they dote on you—they'll be here for another few weeks, you know. Will you find it dull when they've gone?'

'Dull? My goodness me, no. I'd have to learn Dutch, wouldn't I? And perhaps Rietje would teach me to cook as beautifully as she does, and there are some chairs in the little sitting room which need new needlework covers, and the dogs.'

'And my family and friends.' He took her other hand in his and held them fast between his own. 'I have more than enough family to share with you, Constantia.'

'That would be nice. We—we haven't known each other very long, Jeroen.'

'No, but I remember you saying soon after we first met that we seemed like old friends. I feel that too.'

'We'll be just friends—to begin with?' she asked.

'My word on that.'

'Well, I do like you very much—more than I've liked anyone else in my life—and if you think that it will work, then I'll marry you.'

'It will work,' he assured her, and smiled suddenly. 'I've always cherished an ambition to be married to a dragon!' He bent and kissed her lightly on her cheek. 'I have to go and take surgery. Come on my morning rounds with me and we can talk.'

He had gone, leaving her standing there to wonder if she had dreamed it all. Presently she started on the beds again, trying to discipline her racing thoughts into some sort of sense. There hadn't been time to say much, really. When, she wondered, were they to marry? And where? And what a funny wedding it would be with a host of relations to wish the groom well, and not a single soul to wish her luck. She had friends enough, but unless she got married in England she could hardly expect them to come over to Holland for the wedding.

She finished the beds, tidied away the children's toys and games in the nursery and went downstairs to make the coffee, an exercise undertaken under Rietje's direction; making coffee, she had discovered, was a serious business in a Dutch household.

When the doctor was home, he had rung for his coffee when he had finished surgery and Constantia had taken the tray up to the study and had a cup with him. And now, when she heard the faint old-fashioned tinkle from the line of bells along the kitchen wall, she felt suddenly shy. All the same, she picked up her tray and went along as usual to find him at his desk, scribbling notes and sorting out patients' cards just like any other day. He looked up briefly as she went in, said, 'Hullo, I shan't be a moment,' and spoke into the intercom.

Constantia hadn't seen his secretary; she came in now, a small, bustling person with heavy glasses and a sharp nose. She shook Constantia's hand in a businesslike way and then shook it again as Jeroen said something else. 'I'm telling Corrie that we are shortly to be married,' he said. 'I'll just give her these to deal with…'

Corrie threw them an arch look as she left the room and Constantia got a little red in the face, so that Jeroen laughed at her.

'She's a wonderful worker,' he observed, 'a widow with two children and an incorrigible romantic.' He took the cup she handed him. 'We'll have to tell Rietje and Tarnus and the children, of course.'

The telephone rang then, and he spent the next few minutes on it. Constantia, sitting as quiet as a mouse, wondered what he could have to say which took so long. When he had put down the receiver at last, he explained briefly: 'My registrar. It's my round this afternoon.' He glanced at her briefly. 'I'd like you to come with me.'

'The children?'

'Rietje can stay.' He glanced at his watch. 'Will five minutes suit you?'

She got to her feet at once and took away the coffee tray, and ran upstairs to get her coat and gloves. Jeroen gave the impression of being a placid man who never hurried about anything, and yet she had a feeling that he packed more into his day than a great many other people might. It would be fun to find out more about him, she reflected, and raced downstairs again, intent on being punctual.

The round was quite a big one, first in the town itself and then out to the outlying villages and farms, and between each patient Jeroen talked. If she agreed, he had said, as soon as her passport was returned to her they would go over to England and be married very quietly by special licence.

'No need for a big wedding,' he observed comfortably, 'just us and the parson—we could choose a village church somewhere. We'll give a party when we get back and you can be introduced to the family. Is there anyone you want to come to the wedding?'

She had said no and been grateful for his suggestion; perhaps he too had thought of the absurdity of a church full of his relations and no one else. 'Choose a village,' he had said, 'and I'll get it arranged. Is there anything you need to do in England? Things to pack up and so on?'

She had told him that she had only a trunk in a friend's flat, with the rest of her rather meagre wardrobe and a handful of bits and pieces she treasured.

'We can collect it on our way back here,' he said. 'We can stay the night in London if you like, and do some shopping.'

'Shopping? What kind of shopping?' She spoke anxiously, thinking of the expense of getting married and the trip to England.

'Oh, this and that. The groom has to give the bride a present, does he not? And that reminds me, I have the money Mrs Dowling owes you in my pocket.'

'Did you go and ask her for it?' she had wanted to know in some awe.

'Of course. She wants you back.'

Constantia had given a small snort. 'I don't want to go.'

'I took the liberty of telling her just that. Here's my last patient.'

He had turned the car down a rutted lane between flat meadows. It led to a small farm, overshadowed by its outbuildings. It looked shabby in the sharp March sunshine and she sat quietly while he was with his patient, wondering what life would be like living there, perhaps with not much money for food or pretty clothes, and shabby furniture.

She voiced her thoughts when the doctor returned, got in beside her, reversed the car in the muddy yard, and started off down the lane once more.

'I don't like to disillusion your kind heart,' he observed kindly. 'This particular patient happens to have all the money he could possibly need. He's something of a miser, though—his wife has every modern device you can think of in the house, they live on the fat of the land, but he would burst into tears if anyone suggested that he should purchase new curtains or furniture, certainly not clothes. When it's necessary he paints the farmhouse, but only to stop the wood rotting, and yet his cowsheds and barns are the finest of their kind.'

'His poor wife,' declared Constantia with feeling. 'Having to beg for a new hat!'

'A hat, in his estimation, is a covering for the head. Probably when his wife's headgear falls apart he allows her to buy another.'

'How very mean!' She spoke with spirit.

Jeroen chuckled. 'I shall allow you two hats a year.'

And after that the conversation became lighthearted.

Lunch was a quick snack and a cup of coffee before they got into the Fiat again and drove the short distance to den Haag.

'How many beds have you got?' Constantia wanted to know, and was surprised when he said 'Fifteen,' and still more surprised when he added: 'I've the same number in Rotterdam.'

She withdrew her gaze from the outskirts of den Haag and turned to look at his passive profile. 'I thought you were a GP, but you're more than that, aren't you? Do you specialise?'

'Er—yes, I do. Arterial conditions.'

'A consultant?'

'Yes.'

She sighed with unconscious relief. 'Oh, I am glad—I mean, you earn enough to afford to marry.'

He blinked rapidly. 'Were you worrying about that?'

'Well, yes, I was a bit.'

'We'll get by, so don't give it another thought.' He was threading the car slowly through the early afternoon traffic and she peered around her, trying to see something of the city. But she had no time for that; he slid down a narrow street, round a corner and in at the hospital entrance. The car park was at the side; he shot the Fiat into what looked like an impossibly small space between two powerful BMWs, and looked at his watch. 'Five minutes.' He fished around in a pocket. 'I have something for you.'

He had a small velvet box in his hand and opened it as he spoke. There was a ring inside, five large rubies bordered on either side by diamonds and set in gold. 'My mother's and my grandmother's, and her mother's before that. They all had small hands—it should fit.'

'It's quite beautiful,' said Constantia, and held out her hand. He was right, it fitted perfectly; she moved her hand to and fro, admiring it and hoping with all her heart that it augured well for their marriage. Her thank-you was wholeheartedly sincere.

'You have pretty hands,' remarked Jeroen, and his casual tone was that of a lifelong friend prepared to make a generous remark for old times' sake. 'Shall we go?'

The day was full of surprises, she admitted to herself as they went through the wide doors into the entrance hall. There was a youngish man waiting for them—Bas de Bruin. The doctor introduced them briefly, added that Constantia would shortly be doing him the honour of marrying him, and became engrossed in some conversation or other, presumably to do with his patients, so that she had time to study the registrar. He looked nice, with unspectacular good looks, his fair hair already receding from a high forehead. He wore glasses and looked serious. They were joined almost immediately by two young men, house physicians obviously, who shook hands politely and to her amusement regarded Jeroen with some awe.

'I'll leave you with Zuster Whitma,' said Jeroen as they plunged into a labyrinth of corridors behind the hall. 'She's the junior Sister on the ward—I'll have the *Hoofd Zuster* with me. Zuster Brinkerman.' He gave her a quick smile. 'I shall be about an hour.'

The time passed quickly. Zuster Whitma was a girl of her own age whose English was more than passable. She showed Constantia those wards the doctor wasn't visiting, and once they paused so that she could peep through the glass windows of the main ward doors and see him, surrounded by a small group of white-coated doctors and uniformed nurses ebbing and flowing around his large person. He looked wise and kind and rather remote, and she found herself fingering the ring on her finger as though it would reassure her that he was one and the same man who had put it there such a short time ago.

He talked lightly about his work as they drove back to Delft and it wasn't until he stopped before the house that she said a little sharply: 'You didn't tell me that you were a Professor of Medicine.'

'Ah—I was wondering what it was that had put a poker down your back. It didn't seem all that important.'

His voice was so placid that she forgave him at once. 'I didn't mean to be cross,' she told him contritely, 'only I don't know very much about you…'

'Only what Mrs Dowling told you.' They laughed together and went indoors.

The children were flatteringly delighted when they heard the news—they examined the ring, discussed the wedding and could hardly eat their tea for excitement. And Rietje and Tarnus were pleased too. Tarnus seemed to be about the house quite often—the thought crossed Constantia's mind as she accepted his dignified congratulations, but of course there was a great deal of silver to keep clean and she had come upon him only the day before, cleaning the doctor's shoes. He had explained apologetically that he had a little time in hand before he left.

She had thought how kind and hardworking he was. When they were married she would see if it were possible to get a daily help, someone to clean the shoes and the floors and do the rough work; she had never seen Rietje doing that, and yet there was never a speck of dust. She frowned at the thought and Jeroen, sitting across the table from her with the children between them, asked quickly: 'What's the matter, my dear?'

'I was just wondering how Rietje managed—the floors and furniture, they're always
spotless—she must be worn out. I—I don't
want to interfere, but perhaps if you suggested
to her that I could do some of it.'

He didn't answer her for a moment and then
said carelessly: 'I'll speak to her, if you like—
she likes you very much, so it shouldn't be too
difficult to persuade her. I'm going to telephone these brats' mother, would you like to
come with us?'

She went, wanting to be part of the family
as quickly as possible.

Regina, the doctor's elder sister, was in Cal-
ifornia, the children had told her that, while her
husband negotiated big business there. The
doctor leaned against his desk, waiting for the
call to come through.

'You'll like Gina,' he told Constantia, 'she's
older than you but great fun—they should be
home soon.'

He began an unhurried conversation into the
telephone, and when he had finished beckoned
Paul and then Pieter, and finally Elisabeth. All
three of them talked for some minutes and

Constantia's mind boggled at the expense, and even when Elisabeth was finally prised loose from the receiver she herself was beckoned.

'Here is Constantia,' said Jeroen, and put the receiver to her ear.

Regina sounded a dear, and nothing could have been kinder than her welcome into the family. Constantia, put at her ease, chatted for some minutes and then suddenly bethought herself of the time and raised conscience-stricken eyes to Jeroen, who laughed gently, took the receiver from her and talked himself for at least another three or four minutes.

He was called out shortly after that and she saw the children to their beds and then went to set the table for dinner. Rietje, apparently inspired by the news of the engagement, had surpassed herself; there was lobster soup on the Aga, *Oeuf poché Carème* in the fridge with a crisp salad, and profiteroles with a dish of cream beside them. Such a splendid meal justified her best dress—a velvet skirt and little matching waistcoat in sapphire blue, with a cream silk blouse. She was on her way down the staircase when she heard the key turn in the front door and Jeroen came in.

He tossed his coat into a chair, put his bag on the console table and came towards her. She paused on the bottom step, hoping that he would say something nice, notice that she had changed her dress, but he didn't, only stared at her for a long minute.

'Am I late?' he asked. 'I'll be with you in five minutes—pour me a whisky, will you?'

She nodded and smiled and went into the sitting room; after all, why should he behave differently? There was to be no difference in their relationship.

Dinner was a success, nonetheless; they laughed and talked and made vague plans and drank the champagne Jeroen fetched from the cellars.

'That's the second bottle today,' remarked Constantia, and smiled at him over her glass.

He put down his glass. 'Where shall we marry, Constantia, and when?'

'Well, I haven't had much time to think, but my aunt lived in Surrey—Guildford, you know. I used to cycle to a little village called

Compton, I had a friend there. There was a church... Would it be silly to get married there?'

'It sounds exactly what we want. You don't remember the name of the church, by any chance?'

She did. She told him, and the name of the rector too.

'Good—I'll get on to that at once. Would Saturday or Sunday week suit you?'

'The weekend after next?—Would there be time to make arrangements about the children? Isn't it rather soon?'

He raised his brows. 'There's no reason for delaying our wedding, is there? I'm not on call that weekend, we could go over on the Friday night, get married on the Saturday and return on Sunday.'

There was no point in arguing and of course he was right, there was no reason why they should delay. She agreed quietly and presently, when he was called out again, wished him goodnight just as quietly.

*    *    *

The days flew by and with each succeeding one the idea of marrying Jeroen seemed more and more normal. Constantia had her passport back now, and emboldened by the knowledge that she had her little nest-egg in the bank in England, she spread most of her money over a hat in which to be married, new gloves and a handbag. Her shoes would have to do and she could wear the tweed suit she had brought with her. The tweed was a woven pattern of dark green and blue and she had found a hat to match it very well; a soft, plain felt, not perhaps very bridal, but its tiny brim framed her pretty face and the jaunty little silk bow at one side relieved its plainness. She would have liked a whole wardrobe of new clothes, but there was, of course, no necessity for that, because Jeroen obviously considered their wedding to be something to be dealt with in the simplest and quickest way.

All the same, she dressed with extra care when Friday evening arrived; they were to travel by the last Hovercraft from Calais and spend the night at Compton before being married early on Saturday morning. She supposed that they would spend another night there and return to Delft on the Sunday; she could have asked, but Jeroen had been busy. He had said something about going shopping, but there wouldn't be time.

Everyone gathered in the hall to see them off; the children and Rietje, Tarnus and Bet, the girl who came to do the washing. The dogs were there too, and Butch, sitting aloof as a cat would. Constantia went running down the staircase, intent on being on time, just as Jeroen came out of his study. He was wearing a sober grey suit, his best, she supposed, and in place of the sheepskin jacket had a camel car coat over his arm. He looked, she considered, more like a bridegroom than she did a bride, but it wasn't any good repining about that now; she hadn't had enough money to buy a new outfit and she had had no intention of asking him to lend her any—she could have paid him back once she got to England—she had written to her bank and asked them to arrange for her to have the money, but it would take time and she could hardly expect Jeroen to wait until it arrived.

She sighed briefly for another kind of wedding—white satin and chiffon and bridesmaids and a church full of family and friends—but only briefly, for Jeroen had come to the bottom of the staircase and held out a hand to her.

'How very charming you look,' he observed, and the rest of them crowded round with a cheerful chorus of good wishes as she was swept to the door in a hubbub of handshaking and hugs from the children. It was early evening and still light and they all stood in the open doorway saying their final goodbyes as Jeroen took her arm and crossed the pavement to where the car stood waiting. Only it wasn't the Fiat, it was a gleaming Daimler Double Six.

Constantia stopped short. 'But this isn't your car,' she protested.

'Er—no.' His manner was as placid as always. 'But the Fiat hardly did justice to the occasion.'

Constantia did exactly what he must have known she would do; jumped to conclusions. 'Oh—it's that nice old uncle again, isn't it?

What a darling he is—when I meet him I'll
give him a simply super hug.'

'He'll like that,' said the doctor softly. 'In
you go—we have quite a drive.'

Their journey to Calais was smooth and
rapid, for they were able to use the motorway
to Vlissingen where they were just in time to
get on to the Breskens ferry. Constantia, to
whom all this was new, was enchanted when
Jeroen suggested that they should leave the car
and go on deck for the twenty-minute crossing
of the Maas. She hung over the rail staring
round her while he pointed out anything of interest, her cheeks nicely pink from the fresh
breeze and excitement, her new hat for the
time being discarded. She was enjoying herself; she had forgotten for the moment that she
was on her way to her wedding, and there was
nothing in her companion's manner to remind
her of that fact. They accomplished the journey
to Calais at speed, the Daimler covering the
kilometres with no trouble at all. Jeroen, she
had to admit, was a splendid driver, which reminded her to ask: 'Is this car difficult to drive
after the Fiat? I mean, doesn't one have to get

used to a car? You drive this one as though you had been doing so all your life.'

The doctor looked as though he was going to laugh, although he looked wary too. He said carelessly: 'Oh, once you can drive one car is very much like another, and this one is very easy to handle.'

They had a little time to spare before they needed to board the Hovercraft; they had coffee while they waited and Constantia, despite her interest in their cross-channel trip, slept soundly for the length of the short trip, her head comfortably pillowed on the doctor's great shoulder. He wakened her gently as they neared Dover and she sat up in a surprised way.

'I've been asleep and I had no idea—I'm so sorry, Jeroen.'

'No need, my dear—I had plenty to think about.' His tone was mild and soothing, so that she said in a relieved way: 'Oh, good,' and then: 'You must tell me if I talk too much.'

'I think that's hardly likely, we aren't likely to be alone together long enough for that to be possible.'

She agreed thoughtfully. Of course, when they were back in Delft he would go about his busy day and she would have the house and the children and the dogs—an hour or so in the evening, perhaps. She would look forward to that; indeed, she would look forward to every minute of her new life.

They had less than a hundred miles to go when they left Dover, and a great part of that on the motorway. They were more than half way through that distance when Constantia, feeling foolish because she hadn't thought of it before, enquired: 'Where are we to spend the night?'

'In Godalming—it's only a few miles from Compton, we can have our breakfast in comfort and drive over to the church in plenty of time.'

'Half past nine?' She did her best to sound as nonchalant as he did.

'Yes—we should be away from there by ten o'clock. We can be in London by lunch time, do some shopping, have dinner somewhere and dance, or go to a theatre, whichever you would like.'

'A wedding treat,' she observed happily. 'I'd love to dance.'

'Then we'll dance.'

'And come back to Godalming for the night, or are we going straight back on a night ferry?'

'I've booked rooms at an hotel in London.' He glanced at her and smiled. 'It is, after all, something of an occasion. We'll go back on Sunday afternoon and get home in the evening. I'm afraid I have one or two appointments for Monday morning, and a hospital round in the afternoon.'

She made her voice bright. 'That's all right, there'll be the children to get off to school and Bet comes to do the washing, and there's bound to be some shopping.'

He laughed outright. 'My dear, you sound as though we're well and truly married already!'

The hotel was comfortable and on the outskirts of the town, set in its own spacious, quiet grounds. Constantia, tidying herself in her room, realized that she was tired. Immediate bed would have been nice, but Jeroen had told her that he had arranged for them to have a late supper in the dining room, and as well as being tired she was hungry too. She joined him presently and did full justice to the delicious soufflé and the light-as-air fruit tarts which followed it.

She drank the wine Jeroen poured for her and when he suggested it, had a liqueur brandy with her coffee. By then she was in a sleepy haze and only too willing to go to her bed. They left the dining room together, but he said goodnight to her at the foot of the stairs, merely remarking that he had asked for her to be called at half past seven—'And they'll bring you your breakfast in bed,' he added. 'Goodnight, Constantia.'

She wished him goodnight too and went to her room to prepare sleepily for her bed. It wasn't until she was in it that she allowed the little thought which had been nagging at her from the back of her mind to show itself. It was silly to mind, she told herself with common sense, but she would have liked Jeroen to have kissed her goodnight. After all, friendship could be warm, as well as love, and she, who had been lonely for so long, needed reassurance of his friendship.

But it was all right in the morning; he was waiting for her when she went downstairs and his light kiss on her cheek was all that she needed. The vague doubts wreathing themselves to and fro in her mind disappeared, and she said simply: 'It's going to be all right, isn't it, Jeroen?'

'I promise you it will be, my dear.' His voice was its usual calm self, but it was firm and carried all the reassurance she had wanted.

They didn't talk much as they drove to the church at Compton, only about the glorious morning and the signs of spring in the countryside. And at the church he gave her no time to hesitate, but helped her out of the car and caught her hand in his and pushed open the half-open door.

The rector was already there, waiting for them, and two people sitting quietly in the front pew—their witnesses. Constantia gave a gulp and clutched at Jeroen's hand, and felt his reassuring squeeze, and 'Just a moment,' he murmured, and picked up a bunch of violets from the porch seat and pinned them to her jacket. 'Flowers for the bride,' he said, and smiled so kindly that she felt tears prick her eyelids.

So silly, she thought wildly, to want to cry at one's wedding, and then took his arm and walked beside him down the aisle to where the rector stood waiting.

# CHAPTER SEVEN

SURELY SHE SHOULD HAVE felt different, mused Constantia, as the car took them with smooth speed towards London something over half an hour later. She was married now, although she had hardly heard the words of the marriage service and she still didn't quite believe that the plain gold ring on her finger was really hers. But Jeroen had put it there, and she had given him a wedding ring too, a little shy about doing it although he had raised no objection when she had suggested that she should.

She glanced sideways at him now; he looked as placid as was his wont and she wondered just what it would take to ruffle his calm. Without looking at her he said in a matter-of-fact voice: 'That went off very smoothly, didn't it? I like the church; exactly right for our kind of wedding, I thought.'

He was right; the church had been small and old, its stained glass windows throwing coloured sunshine into its dimness; it hadn't seemed empty at all. She touched the violets gently and all of a sudden felt happy. 'Where do we go now?' she asked.

'Could you manage to go without coffee? We have some shopping to do.' He turned to smile briefly at her. 'Shall we go straight to the hotel and get the shopping over before lunch? I daresay most of them close as it's Saturday.'

She was dying to ask him which shops he wanted to visit, but instead she said: 'Oh, yes—a good many do. I expect you know your way?'

'Er—yes, I believe so.' They had slowed their pace now as London closed in around them, and when they had crossed the river she was a little surprised to see him turn the car into Whitehall and thence to Piccadilly. When he turned off into Berkeley Street and turned again into Mount Street she gave him a questioning glance. 'Here we are,' he said, and drew in before the entrance of the Connaught Hotel.

'Here?' Constantia uttered the question in a faint voice. 'This is the Connaught—it's five-star and heaven knows what else besides.'

Jeroen was on the point of getting out. 'My dear, getting married is no ordinary occasion; it seemed to me that a mild celebration was in order.'

Constantia skipped out happily enough when he opened her door; perhaps he had been saving up, and after all it was only for one night. They went in together and she was impressed with the manner in which they were received; anyone would think, she decided, that Jeroen was a millionaire at least. She waited quietly while he signed the book and then accompanied him to a lift, a porter trailing behind with their cases.

They were on the first floor; she surveyed her luxurious room with mounting delight and then went through the bathroom to talk to Jeroen. 'I say,' she exclaimed, 'isn't this lovely?' and then remembering: 'It's most awfully kind of you, Jeroen, I didn't expect a treat like this.'

He was standing at the window looking out, but he turned to look at her as she stood in the doorway. He said mildly, 'Well, my dear, I had to make up the lack of trimmings at our wedding. Are you too tired to go out at once? We'll lunch presently.'

Constantia said happily that there was nothing she would like more than a browse round the shops. She skipped back to her own room to do things to her face, adjusted the hat to a more becoming angle and pronounced herself ready.

'Where do you want to shop?' she asked as they walked up Bond Street.

'Here.' He whisked her into Susan Small's, and while she was still drawing a surprised breath to protest, asked a saleswoman to show his wife jersey suits. Constantia, still struggling to catch her breath and making hideous faces of warning at him behind the lady's back, was swept away to a fitting room, to be shown and to choose the kind of outfit she had so often coveted; a skirt and sleeveless shirt in pale coffee jersey with a matching jacket striped with darker coffee. It had the simplicity of expensive clothes and she hadn't dared to ask the price.

She went into the showroom to let Jeroen see it and glowed under his approval and then went cold at his: 'And a dress, I think, my dear. Something crêpey and pleated.' He gave her a bland look which challenged her to speak, so she went mutely back and presently, deliciously bemused by the gorgeous colours and fabrics, she managed to make up her mind to a crêpe-de-chine dress; tiny pleats falling from a round yoke and belted by a cord, it was a dim strawberry pink, exactly right for the rubies in her ring.

They left the shop without her knowing how much these delightful additions to her wardrobe had cost and the look on her husband's face warned her not to say anything—not at the moment, at any rate. She did protest, however, when he walked her into Rayne's, saying: 'You need something to match that dress, Constantia,' and then sat down without a word while she made up her mind between pale coffee kid and patent leather. She bought the kid finally, shocked at the price but still not daring to say anything about it, and when in the street once more she had her mouth open to thank him, and at the same time beg him not to spend all his money, she was prevented from doing so by being popped into a passing taxi.

It was too short a ride to plunge into such a serious topic, and at the hotel her purchases were taken from Jeroen as they entered and they went straight to the cocktail bar where Constantia drank the champagne cocktail he so recklessly, she considered, ordered, and then, resigned to his spendthrift ways, probably because of the champagne, ate her way through *Poulet au Champagne* and a delicious soufflé. Jeroen had ordered white wine for her and she drank this too and was glad of the coffee to clear her excited head.

'This is a very nice place,' she told him as she finished her second cup, and didn't see the twinkle in his eyes as he agreed.

'A walk?' he suggested. 'Or do you want to rest?'

'Me? Rest?' she wanted to know. 'That would be the most appalling waste of time. I'd love to walk.'

And walk they did, into Green Park and then into St James's Park, talking about nothing in particular at first, and then about the children. 'They'll be leaving quite soon,' he told her, 'but coming back again for a few days while Regina and Bram go to Paris. Shall you miss them?'

'Very much—they're darlings, all three of them. The house will seem empty.'

'Not as empty as it would have been if you weren't coming back to it.' He tucked her arm in his in a friendly way. 'Let's find somewhere to have tea.'

She was beyond being surprised when he took her to the Ritz; evidently he was going to cram as many delights as possible into their brief holiday. She ate the paper-thin sandwiches, the tiny cakes, and drank china tea with the heartwhole enjoyment of someone who was making the most of a lovely surprise, and it was over the elegant little table that he told her that he had seats for the theatre that evening—a musical, and one that she dearly wanted to see.

She swallowed the last crumb of her petit four and beamed at him. 'Jeroen, you really are a dear—I never thought…I mean, I thought we would just come over to England to get married and then go back again, and instead of that you've loaded me with presents and that marvellous hotel and this gorgeous tea.'

'No less than you deserve, Constantia,' he smiled suddenly, 'and it will have to last a long time.'

She laughed. 'Well, of course, and I shall treasure every moment of it. Besides, those clothes; they'll last for years, you know—good clothes always do. I shan't need anything for ages.'

'Well, we'll see about that. Shall we walk back or have a taxi?'

'Walk.' She was positive about that; she wasn't going to add a penny to the vast amount he must have spent, and taxis were dear these days.

At the hotel Jeroen suggested that she might like to go to her room. 'We'll meet in the cock-tail bar at half past six,' he told her, 'and wear your pretty dress. The theatre doesn't start until half past eight, so we shall have plenty of time to dine.'

She would have liked to have stayed with him for a little longer, but she didn't dispute the point; perhaps he had had enough of her company for the moment—even good friends wanted a rest from each other's society. She went up to her room, had a bath and dressed without haste. She was quite pleased with the result when she looked in the mirror in her room; her hair had gone up without a hitch and her new lipstick was just right with the soft pink of the new dress. She went down to the cocktail bar, wishing Jeroen had been with her. But she need not have worried; he was there, waiting for her and in a dinner jacket too. She hadn't expected that and told him so, adding: 'You look very handsome, you know, Jeroen.'

He thanked her, his lips twitching faintly. 'I can't call you handsome, my dear, you're too small and pretty for that; I'll say that you're the most beautiful dragon I've ever seen.'

She wrinkled her nose at him, laughing, and from that moment the evening was a success. Champagne cocktails again and then dinner in

the restaurant. Hors d'oeuvres this time, followed by sole and a salad, and rounded off
with millefeuille. They drank champagne too,
and then sat too long over their coffee so that
they had to hurry to the theatre. In the taxi
Constantia tried to thank Jeroen again.

'I've never had such a heavenly time,' she
told him. 'I'll never, never forget it—you're
sure it's not boring you?'

He picked up her hand as it lay on her silken
lap. 'I have never felt less bored in my life,'
and then: 'I should have bought you a fur
coat.'

She was anxious at once. 'Oh, does my winter coat look odd? It was lucky I packed it...I
can take it off the minute we get to the theatre.
And you're not to buy me another thing.'

His, 'No, my dear,' was so meek that she
had to laugh.

The show was good, and besides that she
knew that she looked nice and had one of, if
not the handsomest escort in the theatre. She
returned to the hotel in a pleasant haze of excitement and tiredness and happiness, only
dimmed a little when Jeroen bade her good-

night in the foyer, explaining that he had a letter to write. She thanked him quietly once more, adding: 'And thank you too, Jeroen, for quite the nicest wedding day any girl could have.'

Her hand was in his and just for a moment his grip was so fierce that she winced, but he let it go almost at once with a pleasant: 'I enjoyed it too, my dear. I hope you sleep well. Shall we go down to breakfast?'

She nodded, and nodded again at his, 'Nine o'clock?' and went on up the stairs this time. She looked round when she reached the gallery above. He was still standing at the foot of the stairs, staring up at her.

The day had gone too fast, she thought, sitting beside him as he drove out of London towards Dover. They had roamed the city streets, wandered through the parks and lunched, finally, at the Savoy River Restaurant, where they had eaten lobster mousse, followed by guinea-fowl and *foie-gras*, rounding off these delights with a milk pudding which Constantia had declared

should have had another name, it was so delicious.

And afterwards they had walked along the
Embankment, talking about nothing much, and
then found their way back to the Connaught
where they got into the car once more. And
now they were well on their way home, Constantia sat quietly; they had left the outskirts
of the city behind at last, but the country
wasn't very interesting.

She turned her attention to her companion,
watching his hand resting lightly on the
gears—a large hand, beautifully kept, with the
wedding ring on its fourth finger and a glimpse
of a watch beneath a spotless cuff. She
frowned a little; the watch was a very good
one, paper-thin gold on a crocodile strap—perhaps it had been a present from that nice old
man who allowed him to live in his house. She
dismissed the thought and went on looking at
the hand. Strong and firm and gentle too; just
looking at it made her feel certain that the future was going to be secure and…she paused
in thought. It would be happy, too. She smiled

to herself and asked: 'What time do we get home?'

She couldn't see the sudden gleam in the doctor's eyes. 'Seven o'clock—half past, it rather depends on the traffic. I told Rietje to let the children stay up provided that they were bathed and ready for bed.'

He slowed the car's race through Canterbury and when they were clear of the town turned off the road after a few miles.

'Why are we going to a place called Pett Bottom?' asked Constantia.

'There's an inn there—the Duck—I've been there before. I believe they'll give us tea.'

It was a charming little place and they had their tea, sitting by a wood fire, but they didn't sit long over it; there was the Hovercraft to catch on time, although Dover was a bare fourteen miles away now.

This time Constantia was determined to keep awake, a resolution which was wasted upon her companion, for with a nicely worded excuse, he got a handful of papers out of the briefcase he had taken from the car and began reading them, leaving Constantia free to close her eyes should she so wish. A quite uncalled-for indignation caused her to be more wide awake than she had been for hours.

But she couldn't remain indignant for long. They were on the point of landing when he remarked: 'There's one thing I like about you, my dear, you don't chatter.'

He drove to Delft very fast; it was barely seven o'clock when he drew up outside the house in Oude Delft. Its door was flung wide as he went to help Constantia get out, and the children spilled out on to the step shouting and laughing, delighted to see them back again. And Rietje and Tarnus were in the hall too, and hovering in the background, Bet. Constantia thought she saw movement at the back of the hall too, but by the time the boys had shaken her hand and Elisabeth had hung round her neck and she had a chance to look again, its dimness was empty. She must have imagined it.

She shook hands with Rietje too, as well as Tarnus and the bashful Bet, and was then carried on a tide of excited children into the dining room. Someone had decked the table with a white damask cloth, gleaming silver and glass; they had also arranged a bowl of spring flowers in its centre. She counted five places and the small, dressing-gowned figures dancing and leaping round her assured her in excited voices that they were to stay up for dinner.

'It's your wedding party,' they explained, 'Oom Jeroen said we could, he left a list of things—you'll see.' And Elisabeth chimed in: 'You've got a new dress, I think you look very pretty—Oom Jeroen, doesn't Constantia look pretty?'

The doctor was in the doorway, watching them all and smiling. He said instantly: 'Very pretty.' His eyes met Constantia's over the children's heads. 'The new dress is a great success, my dear.'

She pinkened, because although she had had it on all day, she had begun to think that he hadn't noticed. She blurted out: 'I thought you hadn't seen that I was wearing it...'

His smile widened. He said blandly: 'Forgive me for not mentioning it sooner. You see, you look nice in anything.'

'Oh,' said Constantia, and tried hard to think of something graceful to say. She couldn't, so she said 'Oh,' again and watched the smile reach his eyes. It was Elisabeth who broke the little silence by exclaiming: 'Please may we eat our dinner soon? It's a very special one and I'm hungry!'

They all started to talk again and Constantia was urged to go to her room and tidy herself as quickly as possible. 'And don't be long,' begged Jeroen, 'then we can have a drink before these brats fall on the food.'

They had their drinks in the quiet of the little sitting room, while the children went off on some very secret errand of their own. But there was little time to talk, for they were all back again in no time at all, carrying a variety of packages, wrapped in bright paper.

'Wedding presents,' Paul told them solemnly, and then joined his brother and sister to stand between Jeroen and Constantia, watching anxiously while they untied them. Constantia had a small china dog, vaguely resembling Prince, who was sitting quietly at her feet; a pincushion fashioned like a strawberry, and a notebook with a pencil tied to it. She exclaimed over each one in turn, touched that the children should have liked her enough to choose their presents with such obvious thought.

'A pincushion!' she exclaimed. 'Just what I need on my dressing table, how clever of you, Elisabeth—and this dear little dog—he's like Prince, he can sit on the bedside table, can't he? And the notebook—that I'll use every day, you may be sure. Thank you all, my dears.' She glanced over to where the doctor was sitting. 'And do let's see what your uncle has.'

'A pen,' he observed. 'Now I use those almost every minute of my day—' He smiled at Paul. 'Thanks, *jongen*, and a truly splendid handkerchief.' His smile was for Elisabeth, who rushed forward to be kissed. 'And this…' He had unwrapped two china dogs this time, vaguely Alsatian in outline. 'Sheba and Solly,' he said promptly, 'I shall put them on my desk where I can see them. How delightful to have presents, and such a surprise.'

He got to his feet and held out a hand for Constantia. 'And now let us eat this special dinner.'

Rietje had excelled herself. They had clear soup, served by Tarnus, who seemed to have been pressed into service for the occasion, and showed a remarkable aptitude for the task, and this was followed by trout meunière accompanied by tiny new potatoes and individual salads, but the crowning glory of the meal was the dessert; an ice pudding which Rietje had cunningly fashioned in the shape of a two-tier bridal cake. Constantia was persuaded to cut it with some ceremony, and everyone drank champagne, the children's tiny glasses filled with as much care by Tarnus as the grown-ups' were.

And after that the children, still talking excitedly, went up to bed. Constantia, coming down again after tucking them in, found the doctor crossing the hall from his study. 'I'm sorry, my dear,' he observed, 'my registrar telephoned on the chance of finding me back—there's a case at the hospital I should really see.'

Constantia swallowed disappointment; she had been looking forward to a quiet hour round the fire in the sitting room, but this was what she had to expect now she was a doctor's wife. She said cheerfully, hiding her feelings very well, 'Oh, of course. I hope it's nothing too serious. Will—will you be gone long?'

'Probably. Don't wait up. I'll see you at breakfast.'

It seemed to her during the following days that he had never been so busy. True, they saw each other fleetingly at meals and sometimes for an hour in the evenings, but there was no chance to deepen their friendship; their talk was of the children, or some particularly interesting case he had in his care. He was always careful to ask her how she had spent her day, though, and she quickly developed the habit of running through her more interesting chores for his benefit; the Meissen dinner service she had so carefully washed and returned to the great bow-fronted cabinet in the drawing room, the dear little chair she had discovered on the

upstairs landing with the worn embroidered seat.

'Would he mind?' she wanted to know, 'the
owner, I mean, if I worked another one? I've
never done gros-point before, but I could try.'

'I imagine he would be delighted.' The doctor leaned back and put a hand up to his face.
'He's particularly fond of that chair.'

'Oh, well, I'll do it—I'd like to do something for him. When shall I meet him?'

'I hope quite soon, Constantia. Did I tell you
that the children's mother will be coming
home next week? I thought we might have a
dinner party for her and Bram. But first of all
there's to be a family party in our honour.'

'Oh—I hope your family will like me,
Jeroen, and—and can we afford a dinner
party?' She frowned faintly: 'Will there be a
lot of guests?'

He smiled a little. 'Let me see: Tante Wil-
helmina and Oom Jorus, Tante Elisabeth and
Oom Dirk, Great-Aunt Julia and Great-Uncle
Laurentius, Grandmother van der Giessen,
cousins Landrof, Bartholina, Adilia, Hestia and
Cyro, sisters Regina and Juditha, brothers

Marre and Renaut, and then of course there are…'

'Jeroen,' Constantia besought him, 'for heaven's sake—I'll never remember their names! However many more…'

'You wanted a family,' he observed mildly.

'Oh, indeed I do, only to meet them all at once like that! What shall I wear? My lovely new dress—would that do?'

'It will do delightfully. The reception for our wedding will be at Grandmother's house in den Haag.'

'You won't leave me alone, will you?' she asked him anxiously, and was soothed by his calm, 'No, my dear, I won't do that.'

But even if she didn't see him very often to talk to, Constantia found her days happy enough. She enjoyed looking after the lovely old house, seeing that the children got to school and ate their meals and did their home-work in the evenings, and most of all she en-joyed the evenings when they gathered in the nursery and played cards or Spillikins or Mo-nopoly, and always, even if it was only for a few minutes, Jeroen joined them, sitting round

the table with them all, joining in whatever
game they were playing. But he wasn't always
in to dinner; lectures and meetings and con-
sultations were all too frequent, so that Constantia spent lonely evenings after the children
were in bed, working carefully at her gros-
point, watching television and trying to understand what was being said.

She was making a little progress with the
language now, going shopping with Rietje,
twisting her tongue round some of the out-
landish words. There was plenty to occupy her
days, she told herself bracingly; she had her
family now and a house to run, although Rietje
still did most of that. But she was learning fast,
and spent hours in the kitchen watching the
housekeeper cooking, and when Rietje had
gone in the evenings, trying her hand at some
of the easier dishes.

She had had letters to write, too, answers to
the letters she had had from Jeroen's family.
They had been kind and welcoming and completely uncurious, accepting her as Jeroen's
wife with graceful charm; once she had got

used to the idea, she found that she was looking forward to meeting them all.

But first she was to meet Regina and her husband, for they would come for the children as soon as they returned to Holland. They were to arrive in the afternoon, spend the night and then take the children with them on the following morning, back to den Haag where they lived. Constantia, the excited children packed off to school, went anxiously round the house making sure that everything was just so. Jeroen had gone to his surgery, but she would see him presently when they had coffee together, and make sure that everything was just as he would like it. But when she asked him, looking anxious, he only laughed and told her that everything was quite perfect and not to worry.

'You'll like Regina,' he told her reassuringly, 'she's like a grown-up Elisabeth, and Bram is one of those quiet men one feels at home with instantly.'

She watched him leave the house to do his round and hoped most fervently that he hadn't said that to comfort her.

Down in the kitchen, helping Rietje with the preparations for dinner that evening, she wondered uneasily if the meal wasn't costing far too much; it was an occasion, certainly, but Rietje seemed to be using a great deal of butter and cream, and there were new potatoes at a fantastic price, as well as asparagus, and surely a couple of chickens would have been cheaper than the great roll of beef which the housekeeper was preparing so carefully? Constantia wished that Jeroen would tell her just how much his income was so that she might economise a little. Not that Rietje was extravagant, but Jeroen kept a good table and seemed unworried at its cost. Possibly his sister had made some arrangement for the children when they had come to live with him, and certainly they ate enough for a small army, just as healthy children should. Her brow wrinkled in thought, Constantia began to make a milk pudding for the children's dinner.

She had something on a tray herself, before they got back from school, because for the life of her she couldn't have swallowed the wholesome casserole that had been simmering on the

Aga all the morning; in any case there wouldn't have been much time, for Elisabeth insisted on wearing her best dress and the boys had to be coaxed into brushing their hair and scrubbing their fingernails before they went back to school.

'Mama and Papa will be here when we get home?' asked Elisabeth anxiously, and Constantia assured her that they would. And it was to be hoped that Jeroen would be home too; meeting her sister-in-law without his support was a daunting thought.

She need not have worried, for Jeroen arrived home an hour later, greeted her unhurriedly and went equally unhurriedly to his study and then to his room, while she sat in the drawing room, fidgeting and nipping to one or other of the windows to make sure the visitors weren't arriving.

His appearance, immaculate and calm, did much to soothe her, indeed she was deep in some tale or other about the children when the door bell echoed faintly in the hall. She broke off in the middle of a sentence and said breathlessly: 'Oh, Jeroen, they're here…'

He smiled as he got up, pulling her out of her chair and keeping her hand in his. 'Come and meet them, Constantia, they will...' he paused, 'love you.'

She hadn't been loved for a long time—oh, young men had fallen for her, but that wasn't quite the same thing. The way Jeroen had said it spelled security and content, and a feeling of being wanted. It spelled excitement too, due, she felt, to the occasion.

Tarnus, who seemed to spend more and more time cleaning the silver these days, was already at the door and judging by the pleased looks on the faces of the visitors he was well known to them, but he melted discreetly into the background as the doctor, with Constantia in tow, strode across the hall. Jeroen let her go for a moment, then, because the girl who ran to meet them was quite obviously going to throw herself into his arms; but only for a moment. Constantia's hand was grasped once more as Jeroen said: 'Gina, how nice to see you again. This is Constantia—I telephoned you...' He gave her a bright glance as he said it and his sister grinned back at him and then turned to Constantia.

'I've heard all about you, and I've been longing to meet you,' she said warmly, and her kiss was warm too. And Bram, a thick-set man of middle height with an open, good-looking face, gave her a hug and a kiss just as warm. Constantia felt all her small, niggling doubts melt away; she was going to like these two members of her new family at any rate, and she hoped that they would like her.

There was tea ready in the drawing room. Constantia, a little shy but composed, poured it from the Georgian teapot into the delicate cups and Tarnus once again appeared to hand them round; he handed the tiny sandwiches and little cakes Rietje had made, too, and then disappeared again rather like a good-natured genie out of a bottle.

They had barely finished when three pairs of urgent feet came racing across the floor and into the drawing room, and with delighted cries of Mama! and Papa! the children flung themselves on their parents.

It was quite some time before the first excitement had died down a little and Constantia offered to take Regina to her room. Elisabeth went too, of course; they mounted the staircase together, all three holding hands, and went along to the big guest room at the side of the house, where Regina set her small daughter to delving into her case for the presents she had brought while she sat herself down on the great canopied bed and invited Constantia to sit beside her.

'You're exactly as Jeroen described you,' she confided, 'and you have no idea how glad we are that you've married him—he's such a dear, and I was beginning to think that he would never find the girl he wanted.' She smiled and looked just like her brother. 'I expect you dreaded meeting us all, didn't you? Well, now the ice is broken—there are heaps more of us, but I know they'll all love you. Grandmother is giving a reception for you, I hear—just family, and if you're wondering, we shall all be wearing short dresses.'

Constantia heaved a sigh of relief. 'Oh, good—I haven't got a long one, but Jeroen gave me a lovely work crêpe-de-chine dress when we were in London, I could wear that.'

'It sounds just right—we shall be in something pretty and silky—Grandmother has never recognised trousers on women, so we never wear them when we go to see her.' Regina gave Constantia a long, friendly look. 'You're very pretty, I'm going to like having you for a sister-in-law.'

They were interrupted then by Elisabeth, who capered up to them with the parcels she had at last found, so they all went downstairs again and sat around for another hour until Constantia suggested that she should run upstairs and make sure that the children's clothes were more or less packed.

'I've almost finished,' she explained to Regina. 'I've left out their night clothes, of course, but there are their school things...'

'I'll come too,' declared Regina, 'the men can have the children until their supper time. I hope they've been good?'

'Quite wonderful—I'm going to miss them terribly.'

The two girls were standing in the nursery and Constantia felt a pang of regret that there would be no more card games in the evenings, but she brightened when Regina said: 'I expect Jeroen warned you that they're coming back for a couple of nights in a short time—just while we go to Paris—Bram has some business to see to there, and we always go together when we can.'

And presently they strolled downstairs again and Constantia went off to see how the dinner was coming along. Rietje was to stay and cook it and Bet had stayed too, to help with the washing up afterwards. The children were to have their supper as usual and their mother had promised to take them down to the kitchen for it, and having seen them nicely settled Constantia went back to the dining room.

It looked quite beautiful, she thought, the table gleaming with glass and silver and the flowers she had arranged with such care in its centre. She wanted everything to be perfect; to let Jeroen down would be something she couldn't bear to think about. Presently, the children in bed, the four of them had their drinks and sat down to dinner. And a gay meal it proved to be with Tarnus serving, something Constantia hadn't expected, and it must have shown on her face, for Jeroen remarked evenly: 'A little surprise for you, my dear—Tarnus kindly consented to stay on and help us out. I should have told you, but it quite slipped my mind.'

She smiled at him across the table. 'It doesn't matter—it's a lovely surprise.'

'You'll probably get more of those,' began Bram, and then caught his wife's eloquent eye. 'Life's full of surprises,' he added lamely.

And in bed later Constantia, thinking over her evening, felt satisfied that it had been a success. They had had coffee in the drawing room round the great hearth and talked, quiet, impersonal talk which she had enjoyed, although she would have liked it even better if she could have heard something about Jeroen's family, but nothing much was said about them and when it was, it was vague. Their guests had gone to bed later, but she and Jeroen had stayed by the fire, talking about nothing much until at last, and reluctantly, she had said that she must go to bed too.

Jeroen had gone to the foot of the staircase with her, saying that he would get some work done before he went upstairs, and she had told him that the evening had been lovely and thanked him for getting Tarnus to help. 'He seems to be here a lot,' she ventured, 'but if your—your relation doesn't mind…'

'He's a very obliging man,' he had assured her blandly. 'You're happy, Constantia?'

'Oh, yes.' She stared up at his placid face. 'I really am—I've never been so happy.'

'I'm glad. I really think that we must arrange for you to see the house's owner quite soon now. Perhaps after Grandmother's party.'

She remembered his smile as he had spoken. A kind smile, but it had held something else as well, but she wasn't sure what it had been. It didn't really matter, she thought sleepily. Jeroen was quite the nicest person she had ever met.

# CHAPTER EIGHT

THE HOUSE seemed very quiet after the children and their parents had left the next day. Rietje had gone shopping, indicating that she would be leaving early in the afternoon, and of Tarnus there was no sign. Bet had been, done the washing in the big laundry room behind the kitchen, and had gone too. Constantia busied herself with the flowers, the tidying of the nursery cupboard and finally the preparation of her lunch, which she ate in the kitchen with the three dogs for company and Butch on her knee. It was better when Rietje came back, cleaned the vegetables ready for the evening, whipped up some delicious concoction of her own in a casserole, and put it in the Aga, showed Constantia where she had put the caramel custard and then put on her hat and coat once more. '*Tot morgen*,' she said smilingly, and disappeared down the passage behind the kitchen which led to the back door of the house.

So Constantia found herself alone once more. Jeroen wouldn't be back until after tea, he had told her at breakfast, and disappeared into the surgery to take the morning's offering of patients. He hadn't stayed for coffee, and indeed she hadn't seen him since.

She went into the little sitting room and curled up by the fire and opened the Dutch lesson books she had bought herself; she was to start lessons next week, but she might as well do an hour or two's work now. But after the first difficult page or two she put the book down; her heart wasn't in it. She supposed it was because the children were no longer there that she felt so lonely; they would be coming back in a short time and Regina had said that she must go to den Haag and spend the day with them all, adding laughingly that Constantia would be glad to have some time to herself.

Constantia wandered over to the window and looked out into the street. That was just what she didn't want—she had loved the house full of children, the bustle of getting them off to school and the getting and clearing away of meals and keeping house for Jeroen. Indeed, on reflection, just keeping house for Jeroen would do very nicely, only he was so seldom home.

She twitched the rich curtains to exact folds and told herself severely that she had known that he was a busy man before she had agreed to marry him, and now was a bit late in the day to start moaning about it. It was a large house and there was plenty to do in it. She took herself upstairs, right to the top of the house where she had never quite had time to go. The children had told her that there was no one there during one of their earlier tours of the house; it was Paul who had said it and he had, she remembered, cast a warning glance at the two other children. She wondered why as she went slowly up first the splendid staircase and then up the smaller but still elegant one to the second floor, and then finally up the narrow spiral leading to the rooms above—there was still another floor above that, they had told her—attics and store rooms.

The spiral staircase opened on to a narrow landing with doors on either side, and when Constantia tried the first one it opened under her hand. To her surprise it disclosed a sitting room, nicely furnished and bearing all the signs of being in use. She backed out again, feeling as though she were trespassing, and tried the next door. A bedroom, equally well furnished, and on the other side of the landing another bedroom, a small bathroom and a well-equipped kitchen. 'Well!' exclaimed Constantia out loud, and for lack of knowing what else to do went downstairs again.

She had reached the hall and was standing in its centre puzzling over the discovery she had made, when the house door opened and Jeroen walked in. He wasn't due home for several hours, but she forgot that as she hurried towards him. Without stopping to say hullo, she cried: 'Jeroen, does someone live on the floor above the nursery? I've just been up there—I was going to see if it needed cleaning—but it's furnished and I'm sure someone lives there. You can tell...'

He put down his bag and jacket very deliberately before he answered her. 'Those rooms are sometimes used by Rietje—even Bet occasionally, I believe. There's a back staircase from the kitchen—it's sometimes convenient for her to stay the night. She has *carte blanche* to come and go as she pleases. I'm sorry no one told you—possibly she did, quite forgetting that you might not have understood.' He smiled kindly. 'Quite a surprise for you— come and sit in the study while I run through some notes. You're alone in the house and feeling lonely, I daresay.'

'Well, yes, I do feel lonely, but not any more. I was going to find some polishing to do, but I'd much rather come and sit with you. Will you be home for tea?' She didn't hear the wistful hope in her voice.

'Yes, my dear, and then evening surgery, and I hope a quiet evening.'

The study was warm and smelled of leather and books. Constantia, quite content now, curled up in a chair with a pile of old *Lancets*, while Jeroen sat at his desk writing, occasionally answering the telephone and dictating letters into the dictaphone. Getting up quietly to get the tea presently, Constantia wondered how on earth she could have been feeling lonely—the day had never been so pleasant; as far as she was concerned the afternoon could go on for ever.

It didn't, of course; they had tea, sitting by the sitting room fire, and talked idly until it was time for surgery, when Constantia went down to the kitchen and started on the dinner. There wasn't much to do, but the kitchen was a delightful place to be in.

She pottered happily between table and stove and presently went to lay the table in the dining room. The evening went too quickly too; she would have cheerfully stayed up much later, but Jeroen had said that he had some reading to do, so she pleaded tiredness and went upstairs soon after ten o'clock, and as she wished him goodnight she added: 'How nice it is when you're home, Jeroen. We do get on so well together, don't we?'

His bland, 'Indeed we do, my dear,' was most satisfyingly prompt.

And life remained pleasant, for Jeroen was home each evening as well as coming in for lunch each day; moreover, he invited her to sit with him while he worked in his study, something she did with the stillness of a mouse, although from time to time he would look up, invite her opinion on something or other, listen gravely to her reply and then become absorbed in his work again.

Constantia was dressed and ready long before there was any need on the evening of the reception. She had done her hair twice, taken great care with her pretty face, and now, quite ready in her new strawberry pink crêpe-de-chine, she went downstairs, only to find a note propped on the console table in the hall, written in Jeroen's scrawl; he had been called out to an urgent case but hoped to be back within the hour. Since she had been at least twice that time in her room, she had no idea at what time he had gone, but there was still a good half-hour before they needed to leave.

She wandered into the sitting room and picked up a book and made herself read it, although she still took a peep at the clock every five minutes or so. At the end of the half-hour she slammed the book shut and began a prowl round the room, across the hall into the dining room and out again, and then into the ballroom. It was here that Jeroen found her, and his calm, unhurried entry vexed her so much that she had to bite back a sharp reminder that they should have left the house ten minutes earlier.

'Give me ten minutes,' he begged her, and went to the telephone on his desk. 'I'll let Grandmother know.'

He was as good as his word, with seconds to spare he rejoined her, in a beautifully tailored grey suit and a paisley silk tie, as immaculate as though he had had an hour of time instead of ten minutes. He helped her into her coat, picked up his own car jacket in the hall, and opened the house door. The only car within sight was a Silver Shadow Rolls-Royce, and Constantia said at once: 'Where's the car?' still a little edgy because they were going to be late.

He nodded towards the Rolls, 'Here,' and before she could say another word, had the door open and her inside.

As Jeroen got in beside her, she said breathlessly: 'I suppose it's his? Does he let you use it sometimes?'

'Whenever I want,' said the doctor, and gave her a sudden brief smile.

'How very nice of him—I can't wait to meet him. I've never been in a Rolls before—it's super, though the Daimler was nice, too.'

They were weaving in and out of the narrow streets towards the motorway to den Haag. 'And the Fiat?'

'There's nothing wrong with the Fiat,' she declared loyally, 'though I suppose you prefer to drive a Rolls or a Daimler.'

'Well, yes, I do, especially on an important occasion such as this one.'

Which put her in mind of the forthcoming evening. 'I'm a little nervous,' she told him, and added in a rush: 'You see, it isn't as if I were an—an ordinary wife—I mean, that— that you had fallen in love with me. Do you suppose that it will notice? That anyone will see the difference?'

He sounded as though he were laughing. 'No, my dear, no one will see the difference, I can promise you that.' He added smoothly: 'Everyone knows about you, Constantia, but not about *us*.'

She wasn't sure if she was glad about that or not, but she had no time to worry at it, for he was slowing the car now and in moments he had turned into a side street, which in turn led into a wide avenue lined with trees and with beautiful old houses behind them. He stopped outside one of them, observed calmly: 'Here we are,' and got out to open her door.

He kept her arm in his as they crossed the narrow pavement and mounted the double steps to the great front door, and before he could use the knocker, the door was flung open by a very small old man, who ushered them into the vestibule. They hadn't quite reached the inner door when he darted past them to open that too, and Jeroen said something which made his elderly shoulders shake with laughter.

'This is Joop,' said the doctor, 'he's been with my grandmother for as long as I can remember. He's nudging eighty, but I don't suppose he will ever retire; he has a snug little room here and emerges on important occasions—for the rest of the time he bosses everyone from his chair by the stove.'

Constantia stopped, smiled at the old man, said How do you do in her pretty voice, and offered a hand. The old man took it carefully as though it were something precious and made a short speech, none of which she understood.

'He's welcoming you into the family on behalf of the other servants,' explained Jeroen. He gave her a warm smile. 'That was very nicely done, Constantia, and all the nicer because it came naturally. Let's leave our coats and go upstairs.' He cast his coat on to a magnificent chair standing in a corner of the hall, and took hers. 'Unless you want to do things to your face?'

'No—I think I'd rather not look at myself, thank you.'

He laughed at her with gentle mockery and together they went up the curved staircase to the landing above and in through the double doors to one side of it. The room was long and lofty and full of people standing in groups and talking and laughing, so that the noise was considerable. Constantia felt the reassuring pressure of Jeroen's fingers as they started to cross its carpeted length.

It seemed to her as though the talking stopped and then began again on a small crescendo of welcome, but Jeroen didn't pause, only nodded and smiled around him as they wove their way through the guests until they reached the great hearth where a fire blazed and a very old lady sat in a straight-backed chair. She was a pretty old lady, with a high-bridged nose and bright blue eyes, her white hair piled in an elaborate knot on top of her head. She smoothed her silken lap with a be-ringed hand and her smile included them both.

'Jeroen, my dear boy—and you have brought your Constantia.' She lifted her exquisitely made-up face for his kiss, and continued in her soft voice. 'Come here, child, and give me a kiss.'

Constantia did as she was bid and then stood silently while the old lady looked her over.

'Pretty—very pretty.' The old lady's English was almost faultless. She nodded to herself in a satisfied way as her sharp eyes took in Constantia's hair, drawn back into a knot at the nape of her neck, her nicely made-up face, the soft lines of her dress and her capable, well-kept hands. 'A sweet mouth,' went on Mevrouw van der Giessen, 'and kind eyes. Jeroen, you have chosen well.'

The doctor took Constantia's hand and held it firmly. 'Yes, Grandmother, I know I have. I am a fortunate man.'

His elderly relative looked at Constantia. 'He will be a good husband, my dear—the van der Giessens have always been that. And now you shall meet your family.'

She lifted an imperious hand.

It wasn't the ordeal Constantia had imagined; true, there were an awful lot of strange faces, but they were kind too, their owners welcoming her with a warmth she hadn't expected, drawing her into the family, making her feel at home. And Jeroen didn't leave her for one moment; his hand, lightly on her arm, guided her from group to group, making her known to aunts and uncles, cousins, nephews and nieces, until her head reeled with her efforts to remember their names. And indeed, he must have thought of that too, for between one group and the next he said placidly: 'Don't worry about names, my dear—no one expects you to remember them all.'

He was on good terms with them all, that was evident; their progress round the room took quite a time and then they were served champagne, and their healths were drunk. Constantia, who wasn't used to champagne, began to enjoy herself, but presently, when for a few moments they were alone, she asked softly: 'Jeroen—he's not here, is he? And I did so want to meet him—or have I missed him? There were so many names...'

Jeroen said almost lazily: 'I certainly can't see him, my dear, but I promise you you shall meet very shortly.'

'Is he so busy?'

'A very active man, despite his age,' he assured her. 'There's Grandmother beckoning to us, we're about to be cross-examined...in a nice way, of course, but she likes to keep tabs on all of us.'

The evening had been quite perfect, Constantia decided as they drove back to Delft, although it had been a pity that neither Jeroen's brothers nor younger sister had been there; but Regina had explained. Juditha was recovering from 'flu, but hoped to be well enough to have lunch at Regina's house in a few days' time— 'She'll bring Marcus with her, of course—her husband—and Marre and Renaut are still away, but they've promised to be back too—you'll meet them all then,' she had said hearteningly. 'We're rather a large family to swallow all at once, and I must warn you that we do an awful lot of visiting; birthdays and anniversaries, and Christmas and *Oude en Nieuw...*'

'I like your family,' said Constantia, addressing the calm profile beside her. 'And they were very kind to me—they might have hated me on sight. I'm a foreigner, you know.'

Jeroen smiled a little. 'So you are—do you know, I'd never given that a thought.' He slowed to go through Delft's narrow streets. 'You looked charming, Constantia, I felt proud of you.'

She turned to look at him as he stopped before the house. 'How nice of you to say so—thank you. That just shows you what a really expensive dress can do for a woman.' And when he had helped her out of the car: 'Don't worry about me if you want to put this car away. Is there room for it in the garage?'

He took no notice of this, only unlocked the door and ushered her in. 'Rietje will have left coffee in the kitchen—shall we have some?' And once they sat at the big scrubbed table, their coffee steaming fragrantly before them, he observed: 'You look very pretty, Constantia—and it isn't just the dress.'

She felt a pleased glow spreading under her ribs. 'Dragons aren't pretty,' was all she could find to say. 'But perhaps I'm not a dragon any more?'

'Indeed you are, but only in the nicest possible way. Tell me, what did you think of Grandmother?'

They sat over their coffee for half an hour, idly discussing the evening until Constantia looked at the clock and exclaimed: 'Heavens, look at the time!' and added anxiously: 'Do put that lovely car somewhere safe. Wouldn't it be awful if someone stole it—whatever would he say?'

'He would be very annoyed,' he admitted. 'I'll help you with the cups first.'

She had set the table for breakfast and tidied the kitchen by the time he got back, and they went together through the house and up the staircase. The old house was very quiet and a faint scent of wax polish, mingled with the scent of the flowers Constantia arranged each day in the hall, caused her to wrinkle her nose appreciatively.

At the head of the staircase she paused to look down. 'This is such a lovely house,' she said softly, 'I'd like to stay here for the rest of my days, but I don't suppose that's possible.'

'Why not?'

She turned round to look at his face in the dim light. 'Well, the upkeep—it must cost thousands of guldens—and taxes and things,' she added vaguely.

He smiled faintly. 'I could of course turn into a millionaire... Would that do?'

She shook her head. 'You're a doctor and I'd much rather you stayed one—remember what I said about rich people? You're happy, aren't you? You like your job and the money doesn't matter one bit.' She went on urgently: 'You mustn't think because I said that, that I should make a fuss if we had to move. I'd rather be poor and happy.'

'You are happy, Constantia?'

She realised with something of a shock that she was, very. 'Yes, I am,' she told him a little breathlessly.

'Good,' said Jeroen softly, and kissed her hard. 'And now off to bed with you.'

She had pleased him, she thought happily as she got ready for bed, and his family had liked her—it must have been a great relief to him; no wonder he had kissed her like that. She would have to do her best at Regina's dinner party too—she would wear the crêpe-de-chine again because Jeroen liked her in it, and hope that they would like her too. It had suddenly become very important that they should; she would have gone deeper into this, but sleep took her unawares.

Any doubts she might have had were quite dispelled when they arrived at Regina's house a few days later. Her sister-in-law lived on the outskirts of den Haag, in Wassenaar, the smart suburb of the wealthy, criss-crossed by shady lanes, lined with villas surrounded by charming gardens.

It was a fine evening, though still chilly, and the children, ready for bed, had been allowed to stay up to say hullo so that even if Constantia had been feeling shy she would have had no chance to remain so for long, for she was at once engulfed in a boisterous greeting, intermingled with the news that they would be coming to stay with their uncle for a night or two in the very near future.

'We'll play Monopoly,' cried Paul, 'and make doll's clothes,' screamed Elisabeth, 'and teach Prince to beg…'

'Oh, we will,' promised Constantia, 'and Butch has had kittens.'

A piece of news which was received with excited rapture and an instant demand that they might have one of them for a pet. 'Ask your uncle,' said Constantia, 'and your mother and father—not everyone likes cats.'

Whereupon the whole party, arguing light-heartedly, surged upstairs.

Juditha and her husband Willem were in the drawing room, and so were Jeroen's brothers. Juditha was a smaller, darker version of Regina and about Constantia's age, and Willem was short and thickset and cheerful. Constantia liked them both on sight; she liked Marre and Renaut too; very like their brother but a good deal younger. They greeted her as *zusje* amidst a good deal of laughter, and kissed her with gusto, declared that Jeroen had the prettiest wife in the world, and deplored the fact that they hadn't seen her first.

The children were packed off to bed then, and the rest of them sat around having drinks, laughing and talking and teasing Constantia just a little.

It was Marre who asked: 'Which car did you come in, Jeroen?' He was going to say something else, only Renaut interrupted him rather loudly with: 'I'm thinking of getting one of the new Citroëns—what do you think?' The warning look he shot at Marre was quite lost on Constantia, who was talking to Regina and Juditha, but the two sisters exchanged speaking glances over her head; she didn't hear Jeroen's very quiet voice say something in his own language, either.

Dinner was a gay affair, eaten in a panelled room which Constantia decided wasn't a patch on the dining room in Jeroen's house. Which reminded her to say to Renaut, sitting beside her: 'I still have to meet the relation who lets Jeroen live in his house—he must be a very nice man, and I'm longing to meet him—you know him, I expect?'

Her new brother-in-law's blue eyes twinkled. 'Oh, indeed I do—very well, and he is very nice—we've all known him, all our lives.'

'He must be quite old—I don't know how he can bear not to live in his lovely house, but perhaps his other house in the country is just as lovely.'

'It is—I've been there. I think you would like that too—it's up in the north—in Friesland.'

'Oh, that's why we haven't seen him, I expect,' said Constantia. 'Jeroen doesn't have much time to spare.'

He agreed with her gravely. 'He loves his work.'

She beamed at him. 'You're a doctor too, aren't you?'

'On the bottom rung as yet—Marre is forging ahead, though, he's in the Path. Lab.' He wrinkled his fine nose. 'Test tubes and microscopes—they're not for me—nor for Jeroen.'

She said warmly, 'He's the nicest man I've ever met,' and then blushed a bright pink at Renaut's look.

'I rather thought you might say that,' he told her. 'Indeed, I should have been surprised if you hadn't.'

She glanced across the table to where Jeroen sat and caught his eye and smiled happily at him; her little world was quite perfect—or very nearly so. The thought surprised her, because she wasn't sure why.

It seemed that friends had been asked to call after dinner, a way of introducing Constantia to the people she was bound to meet now that she was one of the family, Regina told her comfortably.

'Some of them are...' she wrinkled her small high-bridged nose delightfully, 'well, they've known the family for ages, but don't worry, Jeroen or Juditha or I will stick close to you. You'll be invited to this and that, but just smile and say that you must ask Jeroen...here they come now.'

She got up and went to meet the first of her guests, and Constantia found Jeroen beside her, saying comfortably in her ear: 'I'm afraid we're such a large family that we know a great number of people. Don't worry, my dear, just smile at them all and murmur—you murmur very prettily.'

So she murmured at a bewildering number of new faces, moving from one group to the other and always with Jeroen or one of his sisters with her. It was while she was with Regina, talking to a formidable group of elderly matrons, that one of them—Mevrouw van Hoorn—invited her and Jeroen to dinner, and this time the murmur didn't work; she found herself pinned down to dates, and what was more, Regina was pinned down with her.

Presently, when they had moved on, Regina muttered in her ear: 'Just our luck—sorry about that, Constantia—Jeroen won't be pleased.'

'Why not? Then we won't go,' said Constantia at once.

Regina gave her a kindly smile. 'Jeroen is lucky,' she observed, and then: 'You can't very well get out of it; she's known the family for years. Our mother's friend and a very meddlesome one, too, and indiscreet.' She sighed. 'We'll have to make the best of it.' She tucked an arm into Constantia's. 'I like your dress—by the way, Mevrouw van Hoorn gives the kind of party where everyone is supposed to dress up—long, you know.' She went on carelessly, 'You have the rubies, I see.'

Constantia lifted her hand and looked at her ring. 'Yes—it's a beautiful ring, isn't it? It's the first really lovely thing I've ever had to wear.'

Her companion glanced at her. 'You don't hanker after the rest? The necklace and earrings and bracelets?'

Constantia looked at her in astonishment. 'Heavens, no.' She giggled. 'And a good thing too, isn't it, for I don't know where Jeroen would get them from unless he robbed a bank.' She paused. 'And I wouldn't let him.'

To her surprise her sister-in-law leaned over and gave her a light kiss. 'He called you a little laughing dragon, and I must say you look fierce enough at the moment.' She turned as Jeroen joined them. 'Constantia is doing very well, Jeroen—we have thrown her in at the deep end, haven't we?'

He caught Constantia's hand and she felt his reassuring grip. 'She's been wonderful. Regina, I'm going to take her home now—it's getting late, and it's been a crowded evening.'

'But I've loved it,' interpolated Constantia, and smiled at them both.

Jeroen was going away the following morning—a seminar in Brussels, he had told her; he would leave early in the morning and hope to be back on the following day. She had been going to suggest that they had coffee in the kitchen again, but when they got home he wished her goodnight in the hall, saying that he had some papers to look through, and went to his study. She went to her room feeling strangely deflated.

He had gone when she got down the next morning. She looked in his study and in the little sitting room, forlornly wishing for a note, a brief message would have done, but there was nothing and she went down to the kitchen at last to drink her coffee and nibble at a piece of toast while Rietje, in basic Dutch, outlined her menus for lunch and dinner.

The day seemed long. Constantia, washing the delicate china in one of the display cabinets, thought that it would never be over, but Rietje went at last and she was alone, with the evening stretching before her. She wandered around, picking up the exquisite trifles of silver and china lying about, and studying the paintings on the walls. She should have asked

Rietje to stay, she thought, and as though in answer heard the click of the kitchen door which she had shut not an hour since. It was Rietje, and Tarnus with her, and it was he who spoke: 'The doctor asked us if we would sleep in the house, *mevrouw*. He didn't like to think of you being here alone. With your permission we will use the rooms on the third floor.'

Constantia nodded, a nice little glow of pleasure spreading inside her because Jeroen had thought about her. 'That's very thoughtful, thank you.'

Tarnus bowed slightly. 'I will bring you coffee, *mevrouw*, and within the hour Rietje will have your dinner ready.'

It was much less than the hour when Jeroen telephoned. She hadn't expected that, and the glow warmed up nicely again. His quiet, 'All right, my dear?' was so clear that he could have been standing at her shoulder.

'Fine, thanks,' she replied. 'Jeroen, thank you for telling Rietje and Tarnus to sleep in. That was kind of you.'

'I forgot to tell you—I shall be home to-morrow afternoon. The children come on the next day, don't they?'

'Yes. Their rooms are ready.'

He said softly: 'I miss you, Constantia. Goodnight.'

Her 'goodnight' was almost a whisper—surprise had taken her voice. She reflected that there hadn't been anyone to miss her for as long as she could remember; it was a pleasant feeling.

She was in the garden room at the back of the house, grooming the dogs, when Jeroen got back. She didn't know he was there until his quiet, 'Hullo,' from the door. He was instantly engulfed in dogs and there wasn't any need for her to say much; she asked after his trip, hoped that it had been successful and asked him in a motherly voice if he would like his tea.

They had it together and it seemed to her that he was thoughtful, as though he was trying to decide something—or perhaps, she told herself sensibly, he was going over the events at the seminar. So she didn't talk much herself, only when he got up presently and said he

would have to take surgery, she agreed cheerfully, and hoped it wouldn't be too busy an
evening. A forlorn hope, as it turned out, for
he was called away in the middle of dinner,
and although she stayed up until after mid-
night, he still hadn't come home.

But he was at breakfast, his usual placid
self, although a little tired. He would be in to
lunch, he told her. 'The children will be here,
won't they? And I should be able to manage
it.'

A remark which hurt just a little, although
it had no reason to do so. The children were,
after all, his own blood and he loved them.

Regina and Bram came in time to drink coffee but stopped only long enough to see the
children safely settled in. 'You're an angel to
have them,' declared Regina, 'and you're sure
you don't mind? It's only for a few days this
time.' She grinned cheerfully. 'I'll do the same
for you one of these days!'

She left a few minutes later, with Bram at
the wheel of their Mercedes and Constantia,
trailed by the children, the dogs and Butch,
who was taking a well-earned rest from the

kittens, went down to the kitchen. There were *koekjes* and milk ready for them and they sat in a row at the table while Constantia put on an apron and began to make a chocolate pudding for their dinners. It was cosy and noisy and she became a little flushed and untidy, which was perhaps why the doctor, when he put his head round the door, smiled as his eye lighted upon her.

It was amazing what a difference the children made; more meals to think about, hair to be brushed, hands to be inspected, beds to make; the inevitable games to be played after tea. Constantia was happy. She decided that she must be the domestic type. She liked having her days full, she liked the children crowding in from the garden, shouting for her to come and play with them, and she loved the sound of her husband's key in the lock when he came home. Her cooking, under the watchful, kindly eye of Rietje, improved daily, and her Dutch, fragmentary though it was, was at last beginning to make some sort of sense both to her hearers and herself.

It was on the third day of the children's visit that Jeroen came home a little earlier than usual. There was no surgery that evening; they had a merry tea and repaired at once to the nursery.

# CHAPTER NINE

THEY WERE playing a noisy card game when the telephone in one corner of the nursery rang. There was a blinding flash of lightning at the same moment and a crash of thunder, which sent Elisabeth to bury her head in Constantia's lap. And the thunder was followed by the wind; the stillness which had been so unnatural for the past hour or so was torn to shreds by a great crescendo of sound.

Constantia, who hated storms, preserved her calm, administering comfort to the little girl while she longed to bury her own head. It was impossible to hear what Jeroen was saying, but his eyes met hers across the room and she saw the urgency in them. He put the receiver down presently and crossed the room to her. His voice was calm and unhurried and he said, largely for the benefit of the children, she thought,

'There's been an accident—they would like me to go along. I'd like you to come with me.'

'Of course.' There was no point in asking questions, for he wasn't going to answer them for the moment. She lifted Elisabeth to her feet and said hearteningly: 'Look, no more thunder—I'm going to pull the curtains; better still, while I'm away with your uncle, wouldn't it be a splendid idea to take the cards down to the kitchen and have a game with Rietje? I daresay she'll give you some of that cake she baked this afternoon.' She smiled at the three of them and hoped she looked as placid and unworried as Jeroen. But at least she had done and said the right thing—he gave her an approving glance and said at once: 'I'll go down and warn her—five minutes, Constantia, and put on some slacks.'

The children, great cake eaters, weren't too difficult to persuade and she took them down to the kitchen, where Rietje had already put the cake on the table. She smiled reassuringly at Constantia as she settled the children, told them to be good and go to bed if by some remote chance she wasn't back by that time, returned Elisabeth's strangling hug and went upstairs, tearing like a mad thing through the house once she had the kitchen door shut behind her.

Slacks, Jeroen had said. She dragged them on, put a heavy sweater over her thin one, tied her hair into a scarf and caught up a pair of thick woollen gloves. She remembered her shoes at the last moment and changed them for a pair of solid lace-ups.

She got to the front door at the same time as the Fiat; she was barely in the seat beside him before Jeroen drove off.

It was market day, it had to be, Constantia thought savagely as he crawled through the heavy traffic in the centre of the town and then turned off into the narrow side-streets to bring him at last on to the main road in the direction of the Hoek van Holland and Naaldwijk. The road was fairly clear here and he drove very fast, taking advantage of every chance to overtake; keeping his foot down on the accelerator, ignoring speed regulations. She stole a look at him and saw that his profile was as calm and placid as always; they might have been going on a Sunday afternoon's ride.

They had covered a mile or so when the wind, which had died down, started up again and hit the car from all sides, but Jeroen didn't slacken his speed. The sky was pitch black in front of them, but on the horizon to their left it glowed with a metallic gleam so that the fields around them seemed to change colour. She was wondering about that when he spoke. His 'Good girl!' brought a pleasant glow under the sweater; it covered so many things that he hadn't the time to say.

'There's been a bad accident in a factory this side of Naaldwijk. There was a whirlwind,' he paused to look ahead of him, 'and it looks as though there will be another—it flattened glasshouses for several miles, blew off roofs and lifted cars off the road. It also took the roof off a scrap-iron yard and sent it into the air, to land on a pile of scrap metal.'

'People trapped?' she asked.

'Yes. And the rest of the roof in danger of falling unless this wind stops.' He peered ahead into the unnatural gloom. 'The road from Rotterdam is blocked by débris, so is the main road from den Haag—they'll have to work their way round—and so shall we,' he added rather grimly, and nodded to where a few hundred yards further along the road, two cars were hopelessly tangled. There were people there, but the doctor, with a muttered: 'I dare not stop,' swung the car down a side lane, not slackening his pace. Constantia, who had always considered that she had strong nerves, began to wonder if she had been mistaken. 'Scared?' asked Jeroen mildly.

'Yes, but don't mind me—am I to stay with you when we get there?'

'Yes—there are bandages and splints and so on in that canvas bag behind you. Your job will be mainly first aid—if we lose sight of each other, go back to the car and get into it.' He drew a sharp breath. 'There it is.'

Ahead of them and to their left were the beginnings of a factory area and he turned at the next crossroads to rejoin the main road once more. There was already evidence of damage; broken windows, one or two cars on their sides at the edge of the road and débris scattered, but even that couldn't warn them of the disastrous scene which met their eyes as the road curved and they reached the scrap yard.

It must have been an untidy place at the best of times; now it looked as though a bomb had struck it. The doctor pulled the car round in a half circle to avoid a great heap of twisted metal and brought it to a halt. There were several other cars already there, and behind the towering heap of rubble in front of them, people; Constantia could hear them shouting and calling to each other. Jeroen caught her hand as she got out of the car and with his case, and the canvas bag in the other hand, hurried her between the stones and bricks and hunks of wood to where a small group of men were clearing a crazy pile-up of scrap-heap cars.

There were already several men freed; they sat propped up against whatever came handy, looking dazed or lay very still, covered with other men's coats. Constantia, mindful of instructions, clung to Jeroen like his shadow while he examined them, bandaging and splinting and reassuring as best she could. She was applying pressure to a nasty head injury when he said: 'I'm going to give a hand—there are several more men underneath. You're to stay here, Constantia.'

She nodded. He so seldom told her to do something in that arbitrary fashion that the idea of disobeying him never entered her head.

It took her a few minutes to staunch the bleeding; she applied an emergency dressing, took the man's pulse and went to look at the man lying close by—a fractured pelvis, Jeroen had said, and perhaps internal injuries, he hadn't looked too good when they had attended to him and she wasn't too happy about his colour now. It was while she was bending over him that she heard the sound of the wind change to a roaring whistle—and when she glanced up, it was to see the strange metallic sky tearing across the heavens. Another whirlwind? she wondered, and her mouth went dry. She was still staring upwards when she was pushed, none too gently, flat on to the ground and Jeroen's voice said in her terrified ear: 'Don't move.'

An impossibility; he had flung himself on top of her and she lay trying to breathe under his weight. 'You must weigh a ton,' she mumbled, and felt him laugh. And after that normal little sound there was nothing to hear but the eerie whistle and roar of the wind as it swept down on them, sending bits of roof flying in all directions, lifting some bicycles stacked against a wall and sending them spinning, shifting the scrap metal into rending, tearing, terrible weapons flying in all directions. There was something else to hear, though, the steady thump of Jeroen's heart; it made her feel perfectly safe.

It was all over in a couple of minutes, then the whirlwind roared its way seawards leaving a trail of destruction behind it. Constantia found herself on her feet again, taking pulses, trying bandages and holding instruments for Jeroen when he had to perform on-the-spot surgery. She had no idea how long it was before she heard the reassuring sing-song of the ambulances and police; it seemed like hours, but afterwards she discovered that it was less than half an hour. The surgical teams took over then, and Jeroen walked her back to the car and told her to sit there until he was ready. She fell asleep almost at once and awoke to find him beside her, looking at her. She mumbled, 'So sorry,' and then watching the lift of his eyebrows, burst out: 'I must look awful!'

He leaned over and kissed her gently. 'You look like a worn-out child—or do I mean a dragon? We're going home.'

'Were there many hurt?' she wanted to know. 'Did the second whirlwind do much damage? That man—the one with the head wound that wouldn't stop bleeding—is he all right?'

'He's fine—in hospital by now. Thank heaven, the damage wasn't too bad the second time round.' He was feeling in the pocket of the car door and took out a brandy flask. 'Have some of this, you need it.'

'How many were killed?' she asked flatly.

'Seven—there are several still missing, they're searching for them now. Twelve wounded here, and the police tell me that there are quite a number of minor injuries in the area. Luckily the path was narrow and missed the heavily populated areas.'

He held the flask out with unspoken firmness and she took a mouthful, choked, coughed and asked: 'It didn't touch Delft, did it? The children...'

'No, they should be safe,' he reassured her. 'In any case, I told Rietje to rush them into the cellars if the wind got too bad.'

She said almost pettishly, for her head ached: 'How can you remember everything?'

'One always remembers those most precious to one—especially in a moment of emergency.'

Just as he had remembered her, even though she wasn't precious to him. He had flung her down and shielded her from danger in less time than it had taken her to think about it. He had even laughed.

He started up the car and backed slowly away from the mess and muddle and several men waved as they passed, and the two policemen at the entrance saluted him. Constantia felt very proud of him.

They drove back at a more sober pace, not talking, busy with their thoughts. The children would be on the point of going to bed, but she would have to change her clothes before she went to say goodnight to them. She glanced sideways at Jeroen; he would have to change his clothes too, they were torn and stained with blood and mud and grease, quite beyond her powers of repair. He would have to have a new suit. She was still thinking about it when they arrived at the house.

They went in very quietly and she whispered in the hall: 'The children will be in their rooms. I'm going to creep up and change and then go and say goodnight.'

He looked her over slowly. Her hair had come loose a long time ago, the scarf had been used as an impromptu sling, her sweater was as filthy as his jacket and that was torn too, and she had a rip in her slacks which made them barely decent. She had a smear of oil on her forehead, although she didn't know that, and her fingernails were torn. Jeroen grinned suddenly at her and caught her close and kissed her hard.

'You look quite beautiful,' he told her. 'I'll see you in the children's rooms—I've some telephoning to do.'

She felt a little lightheaded and curiously happy as she washed and changed and tidied her hair. She supposed that it was excitement and brandy and fright; it wasn't until she reached the boys' room and found Jeroen already there, as immaculate as though he had never left the house, that she knew that it was none of these things—it was love. She loved Jeroen, who stood there so endearingly large and placid, his hands in his pockets, laughing and joking with the boys as though he had not a care in the world.

He smiled at her now and she managed to smile back, while she longed to race across the room and fling herself at him. How ridiculous it was that she hadn't discovered it sooner, and what on earth was there to be done about it? Would she have to spend the rest of her life with him pretending to the pleasant, easy-going relationship between them? Until now it had served well enough, undemanding and yet solidly assured, and she had been happy...

Anyway, there was no time to think about it now; she joined in the lighthearted chatter and went through to a sleepy Elisabeth's room to sit on the bed and tell the next instalment of the long-drawn-out tale she was inventing each evening at bedtime.

And while she told, Constantia allowed part of her mind to think about Jeroen, longing to be with him again and yet shy...but no need to be shy, she reminded herself ruefully, he was going out that evening, to some dinner or other to do with the College of Surgeons.

She saw him only briefly before he went, and beyond asking her if she had quite recovered from the afternoon's experience, he had little to say. She agreed to his suggestion that she should go to bed early because it seemed the best thing to say, although the idea of lying in bed and worrying away at her problems didn't appeal to her in the least, and she saw him off with what she hoped was a convincing display of just the right amount of wifely interest without being fulsome. Her efforts were indeed wooden, to say the least, and the doctor gave her a long intent look as he went, which she didn't see.

But circumstances were on her side. Corrie didn't turn up the next morning, and shortly after she was due to arrive a small boy came with a note to say that she was ill in bed with 'flu. Constantia, pressed into instant service as receptionist and general helper at morning surgery, forgot to be wooden; she struggled with names, found notes, procured forms and did a little bandaging on the side, with commendable aplomb. It was a relief to find that Tarnus had come that morning and was bustling around, fetching the coffee to the doctor's study after surgery and assuring Constantia that she had no need to worry about anything.

He came a good deal, she thought, surely the silver didn't take up quite as much time as he appeared to spend at the house? She mentioned it a shade diffidently to Jeroen, who looked up from the notes he was writing up and smiled briefly with a casual: 'The better for us, don't you agree, my dear?'

One of those unanswerable remarks he seemed so adept at giving when he didn't want

to pursue a conversation. She said rather pettishly: 'Oh, well, I suppose so,' and then:
'Jeroen, shall we ever have a home of our own?'

He paused in his writing, his face blandly
enquiring. 'I thought you liked this place?'

She put the coffee cup under his splendid
nose. 'Oh, I do—you know that—it's just that
if it's not yours—ours—it will never be home.'

He saw the coffee at last and absentmindedly drank half of it. 'Then we must do something about it, Constantia.'

Her peevishness evaporated. 'No, no, I
didn't mean that—I don't want to interfere—
you're happy here.'

'But if you're not, I repeat that something
must be done about it.'

She wished she had never said a word. 'I'm
quite happy wherever you are.'

She could have bitten out her tongue for allowing the words to trip over it so easily, but
strangely he didn't seem to notice anything out
of the ordinary about her words. 'Spoken like
a true friend and loyal wife,' he told her placidly. 'Are we doing anything on Saturday evening?'

'We're going to Mevrouw van Hoorn's dinner party.'

The doctor frowned. 'I'd forgotten. We can't escape it, I suppose?'

'I'll be ill, if you like...'

He grinned at her over his cup. 'And meet her in church on Sunday morning. Why did we accept?'

She reminded him that they had been invited at the same time as his sister and husband. 'While we were all talking together after dinner, if you remember, and we couldn't have refused very easily. Don't you like her?'

'Very few people like her. What shall you wear?'

'Well, I've a long evening skirt; I had it for the hospital ball last year, and a crêpe blouse to go with it.'

He began gathering together his papers. 'We'll go shopping this afternoon—I should like my wife to be the best-dressed woman in the room on Saturday. You always look delightful, Constantia, but I haven't bought you anything for I don't know how long.'

'But you did—when we were in London— a jersey suit and shoes and...'

He laughed at her. 'Even a mere man knows that no woman would be seen dead in a jersey suit at a dinner party. Not one of Mevrouw van Hoorn's grand affairs.'

'C & A were advertising,' said Constantia, 'it was in the paper yesterday...'

'I'll be home for lunch,' he told her as he got up to go. 'I'll speak to Rietje about the children before we go.'

Den Haag looked very splendid in the bright, chilly sunshine. Jeroen parked the car, took Constantia's arm in his and started off through the streets. As they walked through Noordeinde, Constantia observed: 'Isn't this where all the expensive shops are? I'm sure C & A and Vroom and Dreesman...'

'Just for once we're going to be wildly extravagant,' he retorted. 'Regina told me of this shop...' They had turned into the Plaats and he stopped outside a gown shop which she saw at a glance would be very expensive.

'It looks a bit too...' she began weakly, and was hurried inside before she could protest further.

She spent a delightful half-hour. The elegant showroom was empty save for themselves, and the saleswoman brought out gown after gown for her to see. They were all lovely and, Constantia dared say, dreadfully expensive, but the surreptitious glances she threw at the doctor revealed no disquiet on his face. Evidently they weren't as expensive as she had thought. Only when she at last saw just what she wanted did she hesitate. It was a gossamer creation of silk organza, pearly grey and embroidered with little pink flowers and trimmed with narrow edgings of lace. It would cost a bomb, she felt sure, and turned her attention to a less extravagant dress which she felt sure would remain more or less in fashion for the next year or two. But she had reckoned without Jeroen.

'I like that grey thing,' he observed. 'Try it on, my dear. A grey dress with pearls,' he reminded her.

It was a perfect fit and even Constantia, the least vain of girls, had to admit that it looked quite gorgeous. And Jeroen seemed to think the same, for he took one look when she went into the showroom to let him see it, and said: 'That's the one, we'll have it.'

They bought shoes too, and fine tights, but when he said, 'You must have a wrap,' she protested strongly.

'Jeroen, I don't know how much you've spent, but I can't let you spend any more on me. The dress is lovely and the sandals, but I could have a shawl—they're quite fashionable, you know.'

For answer he took her arm and marched her to the Kneuterdijk where there were more small, expensive shops, and outside a corner shop he paused. 'This is the one,' he said, 'and if it makes you feel happier, I'm only spending some money I had lying idle.'

They came out into the street presently, Constantia feeling slightly bemused, the proud possessor of a little white mink jacket. They went and had a cup of tea then at the Maison Krul close by and she, almost speechless with happiness, had never felt so happy in her whole life. Just before they got up to go she said shyly: 'Jeroen, I'll never be able to thank you. I don't deserve such lovely presents—it seems such a lot of money to spend just for one evening.'

He smiled across the little table. 'Constantia, one of the pleasures of marriage is that one can buy one's wife a present now and again. You are a very pretty girl, you know, and pretty girls should have pretty things.'

Her mouth curved in a smile. 'Thank you, Jeroen. I'm sure Mevrouw van Hoorn's dinner party is going to be marvellous—something we shall both remember.'

The evening of the dinner party started splendidly. Constantia had tripped down the great staircase in her silver sandals and Jeroen, waiting in the hall, had looked most satisfyingly impressed. Her heart had raced at the sight of him, hoping that he would look more than that; that he would fall head over heels in love with her. But he stayed just where he was, in the middle of the hall, and after a moment he said mildly: 'Very nice, my dear.'

Rage choked her for a few seconds. She wanted to tear off her lovely dress and stamp on it, and then throw it at him. That would have been pointless and unkind, and stupid too; he had spent a great deal of money on her and even though he didn't love her, he liked her—was fond of her even. She felt ashamed of her ill-temper as she gained the hall, twirled round in front of him and said gaily: 'Isn't it pretty? I feel like a princess.'

'A dragon, a small, quite perfect dragon,' he corrected her. 'Did the children see you?'

She danced a few steps towards him. 'Oh, yes. Elisabeth says I must wear this dress at her wedding, and the boys shouted: *Épatant* and *Magnifique*—they're learning French at school, you know.'

She spread her silken skirts wide and re-volved slowly. 'Shall I do?'

Jeroen caught her hand and kissed it. 'In-deed you will, Constantia—you're as pretty as a picture,' and for a few moments she allowed herself to live in a lovely makebelieve world, then he had let go of her hand and crossed the hall to where the mink jacket lay ready.

There weren't a great many guests at Mev-rouw van Hoorn's house—sixteen all told, and

Constantia had met most of them already. The women eyed her with kindly envy, and one of them remarked: 'You clever girl, not to wear any jewels with that lovely dress—it's quite perfect,' and Constantia thanked her in her pretty voice while the thought that she had no jewels, even if she had wanted to wear them, made its painful way through her head. Jeroen had given her her lovely engagement ring, she reminded herself loyally, and probably Elisabeth had been wrong when she had chattered about the box of family jewellery which belonged to her uncle. She touched the rubies on her finger and took comfort from them before her dinner partner claimed her. The *burgermeester*, no less; she wondered briefly why she, the youngest and least important of the ladies there, should have been chosen to partner him—it seemed to her that one or other of the other ladies present should have had that honour, although none of them appeared to mind. They smiled and nodded to her, and even her hostess, who didn't smile easily, was smiling. It looked a painful business, as though she had done her duty at all costs and very much against her own inclinations.

Mevrouw van Hoorn's house was a splendid one but with none of the charm of the house in Oude Delft. The dining room was heavily furnished with Second Empire furniture and smelled strongly of wax polish, but Constantia, who had a splendid appetite, didn't allow this to spoil her dinner. She supped her iced consommé, ate the whitebait which followed it, did justice to the elaborate dish of duck pie with brandy and orange sauce, and rounded off this repast with a lemon cream, all the while conversing pleasantly with the *burgermeester* on the one hand and a handsome, rather dashing young man on the other. Jeroen was on the other side of the long table; Constantia could just see him over the elaborate floral arrangement in its centre; she looked at him several times, but he didn't look at her. He seemed fully occupied with his own partner, a handsome woman in her forties, smart and, judging from the smiles on Jeroen's face, witty with it. Constantia felt a twinge of peevishness and applied herself with enthusiasm to the entertaining of the two gentlemen on either side of her. She succeeded very well; they laughed a good deal and she had the satisfaction of seeing Jeroen look across the table at her. She gave him a bright smile, iced at the edges, and turned back to the young men.

Mevrouw van Hoorn liked things done properly, so the ladies retired to the drawing room presently, leaving the men at the table, and Constantia found herself with Regina keeping a sisterly eye on her as she sat with her hostess. Mevrouw van Hoorn wasted no time, but embarked at once on a catechism as to the suddenness of Constantia's marriage, its extreme quietness and the pity it was that she had no family of her own.

'Of course, dear Jeroen has a large family, is that not so?' She turned to Regina. 'So scattered too, but of course in your circumstances that is no disadvantage—he has only to get out that Rolls-Royce of his—money does smooth one's path.'

Regina looked so uncomfortable that Constantia, only half listening, felt quite sorry for her; she was surprised too when her sister-in-law said: 'Mevrouw de Holt asked to have a little chat with Constantia. It seems a good idea if they got together now before the men come in.'

But Mevrouw van Hoorn had made up her mind to hold a conversation with Constantia, and no one was going to stop her. She fixed her with a beady black eye, patted the sofa beside her and when Constantia was seated, asked in ringing tones: 'Well, my dear, how do you enjoy being married to Jeroen?'

Constantia reminded herself that she was a married lady now, a doctor's wife, and had no need to feel shy or nervous of anyone, certainly not her hostess. She replied composedly: 'Very much, thank you.' She smiled nicely and twitched her gossamer skirts just so.

'You have done well for yourself.'

There was no reply to that, whatever she said would be wrong and although most of the other ladies were at the other end of the room, Constantia felt sure that their ears were stretched. She folded her hands on her silken lap and switched on the smile again. It was

Regina, hovering close by, who answered
for her.

'Jeroen has done well for himself,' she declared. 'How is your son, Mevrouw van
Hoorn?'

Her hostess cast a flickering glance at her.
'He's well,' she said shortly, and then turned
back to Constantia. 'Of course you enjoy being
the wife of a baron, I daresay,' she stated, and
Constantia heard Regina gasp as she stared
blankly at her hostess.

'Me?' she asked.

Mevrouw van Hoorn gave a metallic trill of
laughter. 'You wish to have your little joke, do
you not? You pretend to be surprised.'

'No,' said Constantia baldly. She felt pecu-
liar; rather as though she had been knocked on
the head and wasn't quite conscious.

The older woman eyed her with astonishment, but before she could speak Regina, still
hovering, said feverishly: 'That delicious
sweet we had at dinner—you really must let
me have the recipe.'

Mevrouw van Hoorn regarded her with a
cold eye. 'My cook will let you have it. I wish

you would not interrupt me, Regina—Constantia and I are having a pleasant little chat.'

Constantia caught Regina's eye and smiled a little, although it was difficult to do so; her hostess was overpowering to say the least, and talking a lot of nonsense as well. She wished heartily that the evening were over—no wonder Jeroen hadn't wanted to come.

Her hostess was addressing her once more. 'There aren't many girls as lucky as you are,' she said penetratingly, 'to be married to a m...'

She never uttered the word; Regina, her coffee cup and saucer in her hand, had made a quick step forward and apparently losing her balance for a moment, had shot its contents down Mevrouw van Hoorn's back. During the ensuing moment of apology, icy rage and quite unnecessary advice given by all the ladies in the room, Constantia had time to ponder why her sister-in-law should have deliberately poured coffee over their hostess, and when that lady rustled off to repair the damage she got up from her chair and followed Regina to the sofa where she had joined the rest of the party to mull over the little incident.

Presently, when they were alone, Constantia said low-voiced: 'Regina, why did you do that? It was something you didn't want Mevrouw van Hoorn to tell me—and I don't understand about Jeroen...'

Regina looked stricken and faintly excited too. 'Ask him,' she said, and sighed quite audibly as the door opened and the gentlemen came in. Jeroen was with his host, smilingly listening to some story or other while his eyes searched the room. They narrowed when they lighted on Constantia, and with a brief excuse he wandered through the little groups of chattering guests until he was standing in front of her, shielding her from the rest of the room.

'My dear, you look bewildered—what's happened?'

His sister answered. 'Mevrouw van Hoorn, of course. She talked...I spilt my coffee down her neck, but you'll have to explain to Constantia now.'

'Explain what?' Constantia was feeling a little sick and there were several urgent questions she wanted to ask, and she saw no chance of asking them for another hour or so.

'When we get home, my dear,' said Jeroen, and turned to speak to several people who were converging on them. And after that there was no chance to be alone with him; she laughed and talked and said all the right things to her hostess and the people around her, looking like a fairy creature in her delicate gown— a puzzled fairy, if one looked deep into her eyes.

It seemed an age before the party broke up and another age while protracted goodbyes were said, invitations given and accepted, final little jokes made. They neither of them spoke as the doctor drove the short distance home, but once they were in the house Constantia turned to look at him. 'I don't want to talk now, Jeroen, but please will you answer me if I ask you some questions?'

He opened the sitting room door and ushered her inside. His, 'Sit down, my dear,' was uttered in his usual calm tones, but she shook her head. All the same she held on to the back

of a chair because she was shaking with rage
and misery and unhappiness.

'Mevrouw van Hoorn,' she began, 'she
talked to me—she said that…she asked me if
I liked being a baron's wife. I thought she was
joking, and then Regina tried to stop her.' She
paused. 'Coffee down that wildly expensive
dress…' She caught her breath. 'Jeroen, I
thought when we met that you were a GP and
then I discovered that you were a professor,
and now she says you're a baron. Are you a
baron?'

'Yes, my dear.'

'Why didn't you tell me?' She didn't give
him a chance to answer, but went on a little
wildly, 'She said I was a lucky girl to be married to you, and she was going to say more
than that, only Regina poured her coffee over
her. I want to know what she was going to
say.'

Her grey eyes searched his face and found
it as placid as ever.

'I imagine she was about to say that I'm a
millionaire.'

There was a leaden weight in Constantia's chest. Surely if he had had any feeling for her at all he would have told her? Instead he had planned an elaborate kind of game in which everyone knew the answers except her.

'Rietje?' she asked in a rather high voice, 'and Tarnus? And I suppose there was an army of servants tucked away somewhere so that I could get on with the dusting and washing up and imagine that I was being useful and helping you.'

Her voice was bitter, and when he took a step towards her she cried suddenly, 'No, I don't want you to make excuses—I don't know why you did it. I—I don't think I want to know. I suspect it was because you were sorry for me.' She had meant to say more than that, but her throat closed over with the knot of tears there; she gave a sad little wail and ran past him and upstairs to her room.

To fling herself on her bed and howl her eyes out was what she wanted to do, but that wouldn't help. She took off the beautiful dress she had been so excited about wearing and hung it away carefully, then still sobbing as she hadn't sobbed for years, she undressed, had a bath, put on a dressing gown and went to fetch a suitcase from the closet. She packed carefully, giving exaggerated attention to exactly what she should take—when she had finally finished it was deep in the night then she got into bed and closed her eyes, but not to sleep.

Small remembered incidents crept into her mind—the first time she had seen Tarnus, the Daimler that had taken them to England, the clothes Jeroen had bought for her, the faint air of excitement when she had been introduced to his family—they had known, of course, probably they had laughed at the idea of the dyed-in-the-wool bachelor of the family marrying so obviously for pity.

And yet they had all been so kind, and Regina had tried so hard to prevent Mevrouw van Hoorn from letting the cat out of the bag. It was incredible that in the weeks since she had been in Jeroen's house, she had never suspected. The same thoughts raced round and round inside her poor aching head; she had just decided that she would get up and dress, ready to leave the house before anyone was about, when she fell asleep.

It was almost half past nine when Constantia woke. Probably Rietje had said that she wasn't to be disturbed until she rang for her tea. She got up and dressed quickly in the tweed suit she had brought with her when she had gone to nurse Mrs Dowling, did her pale face and combed her hair without much attention to its neatness, and went downstairs. Jeroen would be taking morning surgery still, she would just have time to have a quick cup of coffee before she left.

At least there would be no need to leave a note, she thought wryly, although perhaps she should. She glanced at her watch. There was still time; surgery always went on until well after ten o'clock. She hurried into the little sitting room at the back of the house and sat down at the rosewood davenport between the windows. She had written two notes, screwed them up, and begun on a third when Jeroen said mildly from somewhere behind her: 'My dear, since I am already here, would it not be easier to say it rather than write it?'

She had frozen at the sound of his voice, now she turned round. He had been sitting in the winged armchair on the other side of the small bright fire in the steel grate; if she had stopped to look round her when she had gone in she would have seen him, but she had been intent on getting the letter written. She said a little stupidly: 'It's easier to write...'

'In that case, supposing I read one of your discarded efforts?' He had walked over to the desk to stand in front of her. She got up too because she felt at a disadvantage with him towering over her.

'Since you're here, I'll say it,' she said, wishing with all her heart that she were miles away. Somehow none of the things she wished to tell him seemed important any more, but she would have to try.

'I've no right here,' she said in a little rush. 'I feel as though I'm living here under false pretences. So you see I have to go at once.' She added in a polite little voice: 'If you don't mind.'

He was lounging against the wall now, his hands in his pockets. 'But I do mind, my dearest. You see, I happen to love you.'

She felt her cheeks flame and then drain of all colour. After a little silence she managed, in a squeaky voice: 'Love me—you love me?'

He nodded. 'What other reason should I have had for marrying you?'

She stammered a little. 'To—to give me a job because you were sorry for me.' She drew a breath. 'You let me shop and answer the telephone and dust and put the children to bed...' Strong indignation had spiralled her voice.

'Well, my darling, I had to give you some reason for coming to my house and then for marrying me, did I not?'

'You deceived me—this house...and you're rich...'

'And that was the very reason for keeping you in the dark, Constantia,' he reminded her. 'You didn't like rich people, you thought them to be idle and selfish. I had to prove to you that that wasn't true of everyone who had money. And you love this house.'

'Yes, I do.' She sniffed. 'But Rietje and Tarnus—you let me believe they...and that the house belonged to an old wh-whiskered uncle.'

The doctor's fine mouth twitched just a little. 'My darling love, did I ever say that? Oh, I admit that I allowed you to think it, but how else was I to persuade you to marry me?'

He left the wall with astonishing speed considering his size, and now he was so close to her that she couldn't have moved away even if she had wanted to. 'I fell in love with you the moment I set eyes on you, dear heart. There's no one else but you in the world and there never will be, you have to believe that. You didn't love me when we married, but I took a chance and I was beginning to think I had won, but now I'm not so sure. You see, Constantia, having a great deal of money isn't important to me, it has never mattered except as a means to keep my home as it should be kept so that my children will inherit it in all its perfection, just as I inherited it.' He smiled slowly. 'I much prefer being a GP.'

Constantia gave a small sob. 'You mean a p-professor.'

'That too.' He lifted his hands and put them lightly on her shoulders. 'Dear darling, could you love me just a little? I've been unfair to you, but only because I was afraid that you would disappear out of my life. I counted on your kind heart and your generosity and perhaps, just a little, on the hope that you loved me without knowing it for yourself.'

Two tears were trickling down Constantia's cheeks, and she put up an impatient hand and brushed them away. 'No—I didn't know, not until that day when we went to that accident,' she went on in a muddled fashion. 'I'd known all the time, only I didn't realise. I think I loved you when I first saw you, only you see I didn't expect to, if you see what I mean…'

Jeroen saw at once, and demonstrated it by catching her close and kissing her hard. 'My darling girl, you make it all so clear,' he said, his blue eyes twinkling. 'Where, by the way, were you going?'

She leaned back against his arm and looked up into his face. 'I didn't really know—England, I suppose.' She closed her eyes suddenly. 'Jeroen, darling Jeroen, it's true, isn't it? I'm not dreaming?'

He kissed her again and after a moment she said dreamily: 'No, I'm not,' and then suddenly brisk: 'Jeroen—morning surgery! Oughtn't you to be taking it—you never finish…'

'One more small thing I forgot to mention— I have a partner, darling, he's taking it for me. You see, I was afraid I might miss you.'

'Miss me?'

'It seemed logical that the first thing you would do would be to leave, and I had to prevent that at all costs, dearest.'

She leaned up to kiss him, and he held her close and kissed her back, slowly this time and very gently. Neither of them heard Tarnus open the door, and after a startled moment, close it very gently behind him.

Back in the kitchen he told Rietje: 'There is no need to hurry with the coffee.'

She looked up from the task of grinding the beans. 'The Baron is occupied?'

'Very occupied.'

'But the Baroness?'

'Is occupied with the Baron.' He smiled slowly to himself as he took the cellar keys from his pocket. 'I think that they will require champagne instead of coffee this morning, Rietje. The best in the cellar.'

The two elderly people stared at each other and presently exchanged happy smiles as Tarnus went towards the cellar steps.

And upstairs Jeroen released Constantia just long enough to pull the bell rope by the fireplace. 'Tarnus shall fetch up some champagne, my love, although feeling as I do, a cup of your English tea or even a glass of water would serve the same purpose.'

'What purpose?' she demanded.

'Why, to celebrate the happiest day of my life, my darling.'

'And mine, too,' said Constantia.